SIX WEEKS BY THE SEA

Also by Paula Byrne

FICTION
Blonde Venus
Look to Your Wife

NON-FICTION
Hardy Women
The Adventures of Miss Barbara Pym
Kick
Belle
The Real Jane Austen
Mad World
Perdita
The Genius of Jane Austen

SIX WEEKS
BY THE SEA

A Novel

PAULA BYRNE

PEGASUS BOOKS
NEW YORK LONDON

SIX WEEKS BY THE SEA

Pegasus Books, Ltd.
148 West 37th Street, 13th Floor
New York, NY 10018

ISBN: 978-1-63936-925-6

10 9 8 7 6 5 4 3 2 1

Printed in the United States of America
Distributed by Simon & Schuster
www.pegasusbooks.com

In memoriam:
Alexander Waugh

He held it indeed as certain, that no person could be really well, no person, (however upheld for the present by fortuitous aids of exercise & spirits in a semblance of Health) could be really in a state of secure & permanent Health without spending at least 6 weeks by the Sea every year.

JANE AUSTEN, *Sanditon*

From fairest creatures we desire increase,
That thereby beauty's rose might never die,
But as the riper should by time decease,
His tender heir might bear his memory.

WILLIAM SHAKESPEARE, *Sonnet 1*

THE SHOCK ...

*... of the intelligence was so great
to Jane that she fainted away*

(William Austen-Leigh)

*Steventon Rectory, Hampshire, England,
December 1800.*

Falling away.

Spinning, whirling, tilting, and yet everything in the room is deathly still. Pianoforte. Father's books, Mother's huswife on the mahogany side table. Grey light.

Falling away.

'Cassie, fetch tepid water and smelling salts. George, why do you stand there, dumb as an ox? A bolster from the girls' bedroom.'

'Mother, you were quick to act. I confess, I did not suspect so—'

'Hush, Cass. I can't sit all day with her head in my lap. Go to.'

When she awakes, she sees figures kneeling. Worried eyes, relieved smiles. She feels foolish. Neck damp, bonnet and boots removed. She has no memory of how she has come to be lying on the cold flagstone floor of her home. Her home. Home. And now, with that word, a needle prick to the brain. And suddenly she feels cold. Begs for a shawl, even though she is still wearing her pelisse. She is conveyed to a sofa and wrapped in a blanket. Hot sweet tea. Her sister, tenderly holding the cup to her lips. Martha cradling her clammy hand.

'All that fuss, dearest,' Cassie's words are softly spoken: 'You need only time to reconcile you to the removal. Our mother took you by surprise. That is all.'

The tea revives her.

Her mother is busy working the linen, hands fluttering, tongue chattering. She hears snatches of conversation … Edward's nervous disorder, sea bathing, waters, electricity. No need to be sulky as a bear.

She turns back to face her sister and Martha.

'Mama has spoken: it's all settled. We are to remove to Bath.'

WEEK ONE

All impatient of dry land, agree
With one consent to rush into the sea

(William Cowper)

Sidmouth, Devonshire, England,
summer of 1801.

'We met with no adventures at all in our journey yesterday, except that our trunk once nearly slipped off and we were obliged to stop at Hartley to have our wheels greased.'

'And the weather was kind, I hear, from my mother's account?'

'Very kind and very effectual. We had one heavy shower on leaving Bath, but afterwards the clouds cleared away and we had a very bright *chrystal* afternoon.'

She slipped her arm through his and they turned to gaze at the horizon, her pink gown billowing prettily in the breeze. Never a great talker, he was more inclined to silence when feeling most strongly. With this most beloved of women by his side, the smell of the salt air and the gentle lapping of the waves, he was struck anew by the glory of the sea. It had been his life, his world, since he was twelve. Now, at the age of seven and twenty, he could hardly bear to be far from the water's edge, even during holidays or official leave of absence. It had been his idea for the family to take rooms in Sidmouth, by far the most genteel and gayest of the seaside resorts, and he had made all of the necessary arrangements, procuring accommodation in Dove Lane, a short walk from the Mall.

He was a strikingly handsome man, with a strong hooked nose, brown skin and a cleft in his chin. His black hair was cropped in the fashionable style. He had an open, pleasant countenance. Those meeting him for the first time were struck by a vigour and restlessness; though small in stature, he was athletic and wiry. As a boy he had been given the moniker 'Fly'. His parents had despaired of his fiery temperament, his insolence of spirit. Discipline, and the seven years of acquaintance with every variety of danger which sea and war together could offer, had made him a man. His late advancement to captain, his companion noted silently, had improved him considerably.

'Shall we take a stroll to the machines?'

They walked westward, over the small footbridge towards the fishermen's cottages, the nets out waiting to catch the herring at high tide. The bathing machines dotted the shoreline, with cabins painted a ruddy tint like the cliffs, yet at this hour, midday, all was still and quiet. The bathers had abandoned the beach following their early morning plunge and the dippers had long departed their duties. The only sound was the rush of waves on pebble.

Frank stole an appraising glance at the young woman by his side. Her rosy cambric dress and air-blue parasol reflected the shimmering pink and blue hue of the sea, one of the most striking features of the Sidmouth shore. The oxblood cliffs seeped their dye into the water, creating a marbling pattern upon its surface, contrasting with the deep verdant green of the Sid Valley.

The woman was wearing a veil attached to her bonnet to protect her complexion against the bright sun. It did not occur to Frank that it might also be concealing the effects of her recent illness. She had never taken well to sudden revelations. That announcement of their mother's, just before Christmas last. And on the poor girl's twenty-fifth birthday, of all days! 'Well, girls, it is all settled, we have decided to leave Steventon in the spring and go to Bath. Papa's Easter sermon will be his last.' With no explanation as to any good reason. Was it really to be believed that the sole purpose was to find respite for Papa, now three score years and ten and greatly fatigued after serving his flock with such dedication? Then the upheaval as they prepared to leave the rectory and all its memories: finding lodgings, the auction of the furniture – the loss of her pianoforte, so many of her books, even the props and stage sets from the home theatricals. And, piling Pelion on Ossa, the discomposure brought by the news that the lodgings in Sydney Place would require repairs. No wonder dear Jane had entered a decline.

Six weeks by the sea was just the thing for her. Had not Dr. Russell written so persuasively of aquatic curative powers in his *Dissertation on the Use of Seawater in the Diseases of the Glands, Particularly, the Scurvy, Jaundice, King's Evil, Leprosy and the Glandular Consumption*? Frank fervently hoped his sister would soon recover her bloom. Already the walk must have stimulated her appetite.

And later in the week she would sea bathe, though he knew she feared the short trip to the water's edge in the machines would be bumpy. Frank, mesmerised by the herring boats that bobbed and groaned appealingly on the shoreline, had hopes of a pleasure ride or perhaps an outing to Shaldon.

For now they both exulted in the precious moments alone together, unencumbered by the noise of others. He had planned their *tête-à-tête* with precision; it was an opportunity for her to see in him the same person as before and to talk to him as her heart had yearned to do for many a past year. The affection on his side was as warm as her own. She was the first object of his love, wounded by no opposition of interest, or cooled by no separate attachment. She was the one to whom he opened his heart, told all his hopes and fears, plans and solicitudes. She was as steadfast and constant as the Rock of Gibraltar. During his long and painful absence, an open, equal, unchecked correspondence had sustained them, and every direct and minute information had been gratefully and faithfully received and cherished. Lives so contrasting and yet so inextricably entwined by earliest memories, pains and pleasures.

'The rooms are agreeable, I trust. And not at all dirty or airless?'

'We are exceedingly pleased with the house,' said she. 'The rooms are quite as *snug* as we expected. I made the acquaintance of a little black kitten who runs about the staircase.'

'And Edward? How does he do?'

'What must I tell you of Edward? Truth or falsehood. I will try the former, and you may choose for yourself another time. He was better yesterday than he had been for two or three days before – about as well as he was at Steventon. He drinks at the Hetling Pump, is to bathe tomorrow and try electricity on Tuesday. Oh, and little Ned has been breeched.'

Frank chuckled. Lucky Edward, the child of fortune. He would never know what it was to make his own way in the world.

'One day I will make it possible for you to live with me under one roof,' said he. 'Let it be Portsmouth, with a view of the sea.'

'With a parcel of brats,' she replied. 'All of them perfectly good-natured and as spirited as their father.'

He drew her to him fondly. 'Let us buy fish on the sands, will not that please Mama? We shall have my very own fish sauce. The garlick is ready to be harvested and we have Indian soy aplenty.'

It never failed to amuse her that even when on dry land he insisted on dining on fish.

'And I shall ask Cassie to bake a dozen light wigs – Martha's receipt, of course,' said she with a coy smile.

Frank retaliated. 'Thursday s'ennight, Captain Parker will make his introduction, and I am certain you will find him in life as agreeable and pleasing as you have found him in my letters.'

'I shall love him instantly and without reservation, simply because you command it.'

As they turned towards the Mall, a gentleman approached, seemingly deep in reflection, but on seeing the mysterious veiled lady with the light, firm step, he took note of them. *Good madam, let me see your face.* He wondered about the attentive man holding her arm and guiding her over the shingle, struck by the intimacy between the two and the way the young man smiled lovingly at her remarks. No doubt it was her brother, he felt sure of it.

Sidmouth was suddenly beginning to be of interest.

Pencil in hand, the Reverend John Swete surveyed the scene as his exhausted donkey, Joseph, cooled its hooves in the shallows. It was just the place, he declared, and commanded his servant to remove easel and brushes.

Swete was tall and angular, his gait conveying an air of genteel awkwardness, that of a man of letters unaccustomed to life's more vigorous activities. His limbs were long and thin, his posture somewhat stooped as a consequence of days spent hunched over books and papers. His drawn and elongated face was rendered striking by a prominent nose of considerable length. His eyes, small and piercing, were set beneath brows that arched with a mixture of curiosity and enthusiasm. The mouth, drawn into a pensive or faintly amused expression, was framed by slender lips that seemed ever on the verge of delivering some witticism or learned quotation.

His hair, sparse and white, was neatly powdered and arranged in a manner befitting a clerical station, often peeking from beneath his modest wig. Upon his head rested a tricorn hat, rather battered by his many travels, lending him an air of both dignity and whimsy. A long black coat, fitted with large brass buttons, hung about him like a scholar's robe, while his breeches, stockings and buckled shoes completed the appearance of a man who was devoted to the serious pursuits of life.

When perched atop his loyal and somewhat comically gaunt donkey, the Reverend Swete cut a dignified yet absurd figure, embodying the contradictions of a man who sought lofty truths while stumbling through the everyday follies of the world.

Clergyman, landowner, artist, antiquary, historian and topographer, on his tenth tour of Devon, he considered Sidmouth to be uncommonly picturesque. Nothing, he thought, could be imagined more cosy than the fisher huts, set off by the tints and decorations of Nature – nothing more pleasing than the boats, oars, posts and fishing tackle, and nothing more enchanting than the placid sea whose waves, in gentle ripplings, played on the shore at the still hour of noon.

In the morning, what a contrast! All then must be animation. Sailors busy about their boats, Venus *rising from the sea* and gazing Mars' in abundance – they had assuredly not escaped his notice. On his early morning walk, he had watched a gentleman driving a curricle in the most ferocious manner, clearing a sharp angle as he turned the corner with the utmost adroitness. The artistic eye of the Reverend Swete caught all, or nearly all. He would call his picture 'Western Cliffs at Sidmouth'.

He had bade his servant not to linger but to bend his steps to the easternmost extremity of the mouth of the valley, away from the throng perpetually perambulating the Mall. Here under very high and rugged cliffs appeared the termination of the River Sid.

'You observe, Bickell, the waters are not permitted, as most other rivers, to pour themselves into the ocean but as those in Arabia intercepted in their course to the Red

Sea lose themselves in the sandy desert. The circulation in a mouse is the same as that in an elephant – and if rivulets are absorbed by the sands and find a passage through the earth, why may this not be the case with the Mediterranean Sea and the Caspian?'

His man, long used to such invocations, grunted a response.

'There may be porous shores, there may be immense and numberless caverns which open a communication with the ocean.' The reverend was in full flow. 'Is it not extraordinary that this power should fulfil the office required – that it should absorb exactly the quantity of water, which the vast basin receives, that throughout every year the process should be alike? That the power should be the same in every season?'

Westward from these cliffs, intervening between them and the town, ran a narrow track of marsh. Then in a long line appeared the houses in the centre of the valley – a great part of which was hidden by rows of beautiful elms, leaving only enough in view to give the appearance of a picturesque village. Above the houses, woodland and enclosures rose gradually till at length they were lost in high hills, which at their extremities curved in an amphitheatrical form. The reverend thought the whole romantic and picturesque. He caught sight of Miss Jane, the younger of the attractive Austen sisters, and her brother, a fine son of Neptune, and rushed to greet them with a flourish of his hat.

'I'm sure you'll agree that Sidmouth is the gayest place of resort on the Devon coast,' said he. 'Every elegance, every luxury, every amusement is here to be met with – iced creams, millinery shops, cards, billiards, plays, circulating libraries.'

Frank and Jane exchanged a wry glance. Like other visitors to the resort, upon their arrival the Austens had been alerted to the loquaciousness of the clergyman.

'I saw a smart gentleman take a novel from his pocket in the Public Shed – such is the fashion of the place!' Swete continued. 'I recall the lines from Ovid. *Prisca iuvent alios: ego me nunc denique natum gratulor.* Let me translate, my dear: *Let others praise ancient times: as for me, I am grateful to have been born in these.* Now I must reluctantly take leave of this delightful spot, *adieu*, but we shall meet hereafter and be so good as to bestow my good wishes on your venerable father and mother, and of course, Miss Austen, your most delightful sister. As the poet saith, *Thus we travel on together, With gentle gale or stormy weather.*'

Reverend Swete gave a bow and set off towards Otterton with a promise to attend them at the ball that evening. Brother and sister made for the Public Shed, which was not only a roomy and shady place to sit and contemplate the ocean, but also home to the circulating library. There was a new novel she was awaiting with great anticipation. But by now the sun was high and hot. Seagulls screeched noisily, and the clatter of plate and glass from the inn adjoining the Shed reminded them that it was time to return home. The circulating library, and Miss Edgeworth's latest production, would have to wait for another day.

Jane surveyed the chamber, assigned to herself and her sister, with a critical eye. It was a well-proportioned room, certainly, though the windows were small and the space sparsely furnished. There was one bed, of medium size, and a dressing table. The servant had placed her writing box on the window seat. Cassie's easel and paints had not yet been unpacked. The rosewood oval work-baskets had been placed in the parlour downstairs. She *must* finish the plain work she had begun for Frank before he was sent back to sea, she thought to herself. It was a sudden and pleasing distraction from the wave of sadness that swept over her as she recalled all she had lost in Hampshire.

There she and Cassie had, at last, been allocated a room of their own, a chamber adjoining their bedroom, fitted out with blue wallpaper, blue striped curtains and a new chocolate brown carpet. A painted press, with shelves above for books, had adorned one side and on a table between the two large windows hung a looking glass. In a corner had been her own study, with pianoforte and her dear mahogany writing box, a present from her father on her nineteenth birthday. That item at least could not be ripped away from her, she thought, with a moment's bitterness.

She could not shake the feeling that the abrupt decision to depart from Steventon was an insult added to an earlier injury: her father's announcement, many years before, that she and her sister, still so young, should be sent away to school. Though it had never been made explicit, she knew the reason. It had been to make room for the boarders, brought in to supplement the two hundred pounds a year from the livings at Steventon and his other parish of Deane. The young gentlemen had been civil enough, but the loss of the room of their own still jarred. Once her father's teaching days were over, Steventon had become their own home again. Except that now it was not. Perhaps it had never been so.

Cassandra walked into the chamber. She was of a moderate height, her figure slender yet well-formed. Her dark, expressive eyes, often veiled by a thoughtful gaze, held a depth of intelligence and kindness. Her hair, a rich shade of brown, was, as always, arranged in a simple style. Though she possessed a certain elegance, her attire, like her manner, was modest and unassuming.

'A penny for your thoughts?'

'I'm merely wondering why it is necessary that one side of my family grows rich at the expense of the other?'

Jane was smiling as she said it, but her sister knew that she felt keenly the injustice of the different prospects afforded to brothers and sisters. First Edward's adoption by their wealthy relatives and now James stepping into their father's shoes, inheriting the livings and the family home.

'We have each other, my dearest,' said Cassandra. She paused, then added, 'And it is not entirely true that good fortune has fallen upon *all* our brothers.'

Their eyes met, a silent conversation passing between them in a moment of shared sorrow for George, their other absent brother. His image flickered in their minds, a reminder of the boy who had once been a part of their family, always lost in his own world and now a solitary figure in a distant household.

Jane was not done with the subject of James, nor with his wife Mary.

'Mrs. James Austen is much to blame,' she said, and began to sing softly as she folded the linen, '"The cuckoo, then on every tree, sings Cuckoo, cuckoo, cuckoo."'

'Consider our happiness at the news of their engagement,' said Cassie, with a sigh. It was hardly her brother James's fault that their father had made the rash decision to hand over the rectory, and most of their worldly goods, but he and his good lady, it must be admitted, had not behaved well. Nevertheless, family quarrelling was the worst of all miseries and was to be avoided. Ruffled feathers must be soothed.

Cassie took a tortoiseshell comb from the toilet table and worked it through her sister's long coil of dark hair, then pinned it expertly and secured her Mamalouc cap with its perky Nelson rose feather.

'Do you suppose the Reverend Swete will ask to mark your dance card?' she asked, turning the talk to more cheerful matters.

'By the time he has finished asking, the dance will be over!' Jane's large dark eyes were sparkling in the light.

Frank's enormous sea chest had yielded precious treasures from the East Indies: the finest cambric muslin shawls for his sisters and mother, and an embroidered waistcoat for his father. For tonight Mrs. Mussel had excelled herself with new white gowns for them, cut from the same cloth, but with marked differences in the trim and sleeves, Jane's fashionably short – she wore long blue gloves to match her blue ribbon, while her sister wore yellow. Her mood much improved, Jane smiled at her reflection and at Cassie through the looking glass. An evening of dancing stretched ahead and Frank was home and safe from harm. She had heard that the Assembly Rooms had a view of the ocean and sparkling new chandeliers that outranked even those of London.

At the Academy, Frank had learned to dance, a necessary requirement for the gentleman sailor, which had served him well at the commissioner's houses in Bombay and Gibraltar, though many of the older flags looked with disapproval upon such affectation. Frank cared not. He had become accomplished at the art and looked forward to showing his prowess at the ball, alongside his sisters so uncommonly pretty in their white dresses. What a pity, he thought, that Captain Parker was not here to see them in their finery. Jane's dark hair and wild rose complexion reminded him of a young Lady Hamilton.

In the hallway, Frank stretched his hands towards Jane's feathered head: 'Do you know, I begin to like that queer fashion already, though when I first heard of such things being done in England, I could not believe it. When the women at the commissioner's appeared in the same trim, I thought they were quite mad. And some of my good tars were a little offended that the triumph of our great admiral should become merely the pretext for an accoutrement of ladies' headwear.'

The Battle of the Nile meant rather different things to women and sailors, he noted silently. Jane, so close in age, had long been his fiercest defender and advocate. Her letters, especially during the five long years he had spent at sea as a young midshipman, were among his most precious items and he had carefully preserved them from water damage. He felt fortunate that all of his family were such devoted and able correspondents, but

Jane's missives were of a different order. Her brilliance he was sure of; her beauty singular. Captain Parker was the only man he had ever met whom he felt her equal – no one could be her superior.

Such thoughts occupied him as they took the short walk to the Assembly Rooms. Mrs. Austen demanded he take her arm, proud of her sailor son and wanting the world to notice. Her daughters, arm in arm, she looked upon approvingly. *This* was why they had left the vicarage: to show the girls a life outside of their constricted sphere. To find them husbands of course too. Cassie, still bereaved, would take a little time, but she was young and, despite her protestations, would love again. Yet *Jane*, now there Mrs. Austen entertained high hopes of a good match. It would be a relief for the girls to be settled, and not too far away, she prayed. Not for the first time, she gave thanks for having so many boys and only the two daughters to be rid of!

The season's first summer assembly, that Tuesday night, was generally expected to be a good one. Jane's excitement built as she heard the strains of the violins echoing through the walls. In passing along a short gallery to the rooms, brilliant in lights before them, they were accosted by a young man in morning dress and boots, standing in the doorway of a bedchamber apparently to see them go by.

'Ah! Mrs. Austen, how do you do? How do you do, Miss Austen, and Miss Jane?' he cried, with an easy air. 'You are determined to be in good time, I see, as usual. The candles are but this moment lit.'

'I like to get a good seat by the fire, you know, Mr. Musgrave,' replied Mrs. Austen.

She felt the cold, even on a summer's evening, and, not being fond of dancing, preferred to take her wine in one of the cosier rooms. The party passed on to the ballroom, a well-proportioned and handsome space with black and white marble fireplaces at either end and a decorative frieze high on the walls featuring scallop shells, musical instruments and acanthus leaves. The huge bay window reflected unparalleled views of the ocean, flooding the room with light. A music gallery adjoined the ballroom and led to the supper and card rooms. All was opulence and refinement.

There was no difficulty in *not* knowing who would be attending, as most of the people were strangers to Sidmouth. Mr. Musgrave, a man of large fortune and amiable disposition, known to the family, though not intimately, was a relation of Mr. Austen's old school pupil, Richard Buller. Indeed, it was thanks to Mr. Buller, now a clergyman at nearby Colyton, that the family had become acquainted with the Reverend Swete, and it was *he* they depended upon for all the necessary introductions. Jane cared only to dance with her brother, who had engaged her for the first two cotillions. But even before she took a step, she could not fail to notice that she was being eyed by a genteel, good-looking man. On enquiry, she was informed that he was a lawyer by the name of Rose. That circumstance alone determined her to avoid him at all costs.

Her mind reverted to another ball, some years before, when the very gentlemanlike, good-looking, pleasant young Irishman Tom Lefroy had led her to the dance-floor. They had laughed, and flirted outrageously, until after a mere fortnight he had decamped to his native land without so much as a by-your-leave. She had had quite enough of lawyers.

Reverend Swete was in high spirits, as he approached the small party. 'And how do you like Sidmouth?' he began. 'The sea is to me an in-exhaustless fund of delight. Unlike other immovable objects which (however beautiful) in process of time suffer a diminution in their beauty, the sea never ceases to be attractive – the sea is always in motion, now gently gliding with unruffled waves! Now rippling with a freshening breeze! And now swelling with a tumultuous surge! Lashing the shore in foamy rage and spreading its uproar far and wide. *Et Sol crescentes decedens duplicat umbras.*'

The sisters glanced at one another, suppressing an itch to laugh. It was impossible not to be affected by Mr. Swete's ardour. They assured him they liked Sidmouth very much and promised to take advantage of the sea bathing on the morrow. He bowed gracefully and offered his assistance in taking a refreshment in the adjoining room. By now the ballroom was crowded and noisy. Cassie drew her sister to one side and in a low whisper said:

'The gentleman who was staring at you was an intimate friend of poor William Cowper. I've had it on the highest authority. Is he not a fine-looking man?'

Jane showed her surprise at her sister's remark. 'I've also discovered that he's a lawyer, which quite puts an end to any interest I might have enjoyed in making his acquaintance,' she replied tartly.

Before Cassie could respond, the Reverend Swete reappeared, accompanied by the very same gentleman. He was announced as Mr. Samuel Rose and presented to Jane as a desirable partner for dancing. He was undoubtedly attractive – dark-haired with a fine, aquiline nose, and the bluest of eyes. She noted, with a half-smile, that his complexion was flushed like the rose of his name. Tall as she was, he towered over her and made an elegant bow as he engaged her hand for the next two dances. She vowed to show him her worst side, still rankled by the humiliation of the gentleman lawyer who had shown such strong preferment before running back to Ireland without a word. As she took her place in the set opposite Mr. Rose, she resolved to be silent throughout the ordeal of the next half-hour.

'This is not the first time I have seen you,' he began, with an unmistakable air of confidence: 'You were walking on the Mall with a fine young man and you were wearing a very pretty veil.'

'Yes, that was my brother and I assure you there was no intent of mystery. My veil was a necessary precaution against the glare of the sunlight.'

With such a reply, she hoped that he would leave off the conversation or confine his comments to the quotidian. To her alarm, he smiled and told her he had been convinced the gentleman was her brother and hoped they could one day soon be introduced. Affronted by his presumption, Jane merely nodded. They were silent as they went down the dance and she could not help but notice that all eyes were on them. He danced gracefully and despite his manly figure his hand felt light on hers as they moved through the set. Determined as she was to rebuff his attempts at conversation, she was vexed to discover that the more indifferently she looked upon him, the more amused he seemed to be. There was an undeniable teasing, sardonic light in his eyes. She was thankful when the dances were over, and they parted wordlessly.

Searching the room for her sister, Jane was surprised to see Cassie dancing with a stranger, an amiable-looking fair-haired man, whose conversation appeared to be delighting them both. She sought out Frank, who, with great happiness, informed her that Captain Parker had arrived earlier than expected. It was he who was dancing with Cassie, and he was longing to make her acquaintance. She found herself interested, having heard such tales of Parker; of his courage during the Battle of the Nile, of the loyalty of his crew and his friendship with Nelson.

Frank's tales had made a deep impression upon her and she was determined to find Parker the best of men. All thoughts of Samuel Rose were expelled. Men of the law like him were not to be trusted. She thought with fury of the way he had taken his final bow, just as if he had received a high compliment. She would do everything in her power to avoid him in future. Sidmouth was a small town, that was true, but it could be achieved with the right attitude and a degree of planning. The appearance of Captain Peter Parker presented a most welcome diversion. Perhaps she would permit herself to fall in love a little. She knew it was Frank's dearest wish and she was always happy to oblige a most treasured brother.

'In India, the elephants are set to watch young children and they draw them back gently with their trunks when they go out of bounds. They are noble creatures, indeed.'

'Not the elephants again, Parker,' said Frank, looking up from his newspaper.

The Austen women were listening in rapt delight, mesmerised by Parker who had come to make his morning call and to reflect upon the previous night's ball. As well as being handsome, sensible and good-humoured, he was a natural storyteller. He had such happy manners and good breeding. He was entirely at ease with himself. His adoration of Frank was much in evidence and he made light of the frequent hardships of life at sea – the fear of shipwreck, war and fire – as he described faraway lands of turquoise seas, palms and orange trees. He recounted hair-raising stories of the Nile, and told them of the victory party at Naples alongside the beautiful and fearless Lady Hamilton resplendent in a dress of blue decorated with gold anchors, and wearing gold anchor earrings and slippers embroidered with crocodiles. He described Christmas in the city where calves wandered freely, preserved from harm by a painting of Saint Francis about their necks, the stalls piled high with oranges and *ricotta* cakes studded with candied peel, the lemonade stalls and the kettles steaming with dressed *maccheroni* with golden apples strewn on top.

The sisters particularly enjoyed the tales of 'aquatic abode' on the *Lark*, where Captain Parker had first met Frank, then a lowly midshipman, of decks scrubbed as clean and shining as a drawing room in the summer season and even kitchen utensils scoured as bright as silver. They dined, so Parker said, on pigeon, peas, cold lamb and tart, washed down with good port. He recounted Admiral Nelson's description of Frank, once he had been promoted to the rank of captain, as a 'most excellent young man'. How on the 'dear old Lark' they had conveyed Princess Caroline from Cuxhaven to England to be married to the Prince of Wales, the Princess wearing a muslin dress with a blue satin petticoat and black beaver hat with blue and black feathers. When speaking of the Indies, a place of tropical birds, coconut trees and fragrant frangipani, so he said, Parker described the Indian 'Queen of the Night' whose fleeting flowers bloom for a single night. 'A reminder from Nature, Miss Jane, of living in the here and now.'

Othello could hardly have woven a more magical spell.

Parker turned to Mrs. Austen and reminded her of the hams she had cured for Frank to take aboard the *Lark* – his own mother had granted him no such favours when she was alive. He felt a stab of envy towards his friend.

Mrs. Austen chuckled. Stories were all very well, but she regarded herself as a practical woman, not given to nerves. Even when her sons were away at sea, she thought more of their sufficiency of salted beef than of shipwrecks and battles. Why her son Edward suffered from the melancholy and nervous complaints she did not comprehend. What on earth did he have to worry about with all that wealth? And her son Henry, with his fancy French cook. *She* kept a good, though unpretentious table – pease soup, a sparerib and whipt syllabub with gooseberries. 'A good huswife must not overreach herself with dishes beyond her status and budget,' she proclaimed proudly.

As they talked, the Reverend George Austen entered the room. Captain Parker bade him good morning, observing his mass of white, curly hair and intelligent hazel eyes, so like Miss Jane's. The reverend had a genial temper and there was a benevolent sweetness in his expression. Mrs. Austen, lacking several of her fore teeth, looked older than her years, yet she had an aristocratic mien, of which Parker approved. She was a woman of excellent good humour. Nonetheless his enquiries about Bath, and the suitability of their lodgings, were met with a quizzical glance.

'Are you familiar with the environs of Bath, Captain Parker?'

'Indeed I am, madam. My father, now deceased, took residence in the Paragon for the winter season for the benefits of the waters.'

'And you are acquainted with my brother, Mr. Leigh-Perrot?'

'And his good wife, madam,' said Parker, with a grave look. Jane and Cassie exchanged a glance. Could that be a smile hovering about the younger sister's lips, he wondered.

It was clear the captain had been made aware of the recent family scandal in Bath: the case of Frank's wealthy aunt and the theft of a card of expensive lace. Mrs. Austen saw that she must grasp the nettle.

'You know, Captain Parker, that my sister was sent to prison while she awaited trial. I offered to send the girls, but she refused. She would not countenance such fine young ladies coming to such a squalid place.'

As she spoke, Mrs. Austen recalled the letter her sister-in-law had written from Ilchester gaol: 'Not Bedlam itself can be half so noisy, besides which, not one particule of smoke goes up the chimney, I leave you to judge of the comfort I can enjoy in such a room. Mrs. Scadding's knife *well licked to clean it from fried onions* helps me now and then – you may believe how the mess I am helped to is disposed of – here are *two dogs and three cats* always *full as hungry* as myself.'

'Imagine, my dear sir,' said she to Parker. 'The lace was valued at more than a shilling, so the charge was grand larceny and she might have been transported to Botany Bay! We only thank the good Lord that she was acquitted. But you will appreciate the dismay of all the family when the trial was played out in an overflowing courtroom and the full story displayed in the vulgar prints.'

Parker wondered how the scandal had affected Frank's sisters. This was a family that sought discretion. He knew what it was like to keep secrets.

He suspected another secret. He suspected Miss Jane to be a scribbler. Perhaps she was a writer of novels of sensibility or those Gothic tales that were all the rage with young ladies. It would not be difficult to winkle it out of his friend. Frank was hopeless as a confidant, especially when it involved Jane. Parker decided to have a little fun.

'I do beg your pardon, Miss Jane, but I could not help noticing that you have ink upon your fingers. May I presume you are in the midst of some clandestine writing? Perhaps a novel of your own, full of wit and wisdom?'

Jane glanced down at her fingers with some surprise and then looked up with a mischievous air: 'Clandestine, sir? I assure you, I am not in the habit of indulging in secrets, nor am I much given to the composition of novels, unless one can call scribbling upon scraps of paper in idle moments a novel. My hands, I believe, are merely an unfortunate consequence of that most distressing of habits – writing letters.'

'Ah, letters! Of course. But I must ask, Captain Austen, does your sister's penchant for letters suggest a habit of writing often? You see, I have been told that writers are sometimes so absorbed in their pens that they forget the very marks they leave upon themselves.'

Frank folded his newspaper and stood up, avoiding his sister's penetrating glance.

'Well, you know, Captain Parker, we must all confess to certain habits that become ingrained over time. My sister is not *unacquainted* with the use of her pen, though whether that constitutes the making of a writer is another matter entirely.'

'Aha! Now it is apparent. The captain's cautious wording betrays more than he would have us believe. Tell me,

Miss Jane, if you are indeed a writer, what might one find in your manuscript? A love story, perchance, or a keen satire of society?'

'I daresay, Captain, you would be most disappointed by anything of the sort.'

'Ah, the modesty of a true writer. I see how it is. No doubt you are working on something quite grand, Miss Jane, which will soon be the talk of the town. I shall watch for it with great anticipation!'

'Do not listen to him, sister,' said Frank, blushing. 'He has a most extraordinary talent for extracting secrets, though I assure you he will find none here but the gall ink upon your fingers.'

'Oh, Captain Austen,' Parker declared with a saucy smile, 'I never yet cast my line over a fish that rose more readily to the fly than you do.'

Parker walked over to the table upon which there was a leather drawing case.

'May I?' he enquired and before waiting for a reply, he opened the folder. 'Why, these are exquisite! Might I surmise that if one sister is a letter writer, the other is an artist? How charming, Miss Austen – one would think you had the very essence of nature at your command. The delicate strokes, the soft blending of colours! But tell me, what do they represent?'

'Thank you, Captain Parker.' Cassie joined him at the table. 'These are but humble attempts at capturing the landscapes I have known, places I have seen in my travels, and others which remain only in the memory. This one, for instance,' said she, gesturing to a scene of soft hills and a distant horizon, 'represents a view I once admired in Hampshire, the quiet beauty of the hills on a summer evening.'

'Ah, Hampshire! But your brushwork, Miss Austen – how it speaks to one's heart. The light, the shadows, it is as if they reflect something deeper than mere scenery. Could it be that these landscapes are more than a simple homage to nature? Perhaps they are windows to your very soul?'

Cassie inclined her head in a polite but distant gesture, her fingers lightly tracing the edge of the table: 'You are too kind, Captain Parker. I assure you, these are but attempts at capturing a fleeting moment – a passing scene. There is little to be found in them beyond what is seen with the eye.'

'But the eye, Miss Cassandra, is often the most unreliable of judges, is it not? I would hazard that the hand which painted such gentle landscapes must have a heart that shares in their quiet grace. Surely there is more to these paintings than meets the eye.'

'Perhaps, Captain, but if there is more, it is not for me to say. I paint, as one would walk or breathe, without expectation of anything other than the act itself. The landscapes you see are a reflection of my own memories and musings, not of anything more fanciful or dramatic.' Her voice softened. 'But I thank you for your words. It is a kindness to receive such compliments, though I must confess, I find little joy in them at present.'

Jane, meanwhile, had taken up her needle. She had been working handkerchiefs for Frank, and Parker looked with envy at the delicacy of the satin stitching. He took a great interest in muslin, especially Indian white work.

'I never tire of discussing the merit of cambric versus muslin, or the price per yard, though I have no sisters. Are you acquainted with Mrs. Mussel of Bath?'

'Indeed, sir,' said Jane. 'She makes our summer gowns and cloaks.'

'Do you not feel that she is better with dark colours and does not succeed with lighter colours?' Parker asked with great animation. He particularly admired Miss Jane's new yellow and white cloud dress, though adding that on the whole he disliked coloured gowns, preferring plain or spotted white. He was interested in how much it cost to send out their laundry. No detail escaped his notice, though he was never indecorous, merely curious.

Jane, shy in company other than her own family circle, found him most congenial. Herself occasionally sharp-tongued, she detected an ally in his own satirical bent. She prudently kept her thoughts to herself, and to her sister, yet could not help laughing when he described the outlandish modes of the wealthy but vulgar Miss Tavistocks, who had descended upon the town. Their bright gowns of coloured satin bedecked with layers of expensive lace horrified him, and he compared them unfavourably with the tropical birds of paradise that once adorned his garden: 'The Miss Tavistocks' shiny purple gowns do not become their complexions, nor their figures. Indeed, they resemble nothing less than a brace of aubergines.'

'Captain Parker, you must not speak so,' said Jane, trying to conceal her laughter. It really was his tone of affected indifference that made it so difficult to reprimand him.

'And as for the mother with the fat neck, now there's a madam who's broad at the beam, as we seadogs say.'

They begged him to desist. Delightful as it was, such excess of indecorum was not to be borne. They turned instead to the invitation just received from Reverend Swete to visit his seat, Oxton House, which, he had assured them, was one of the gems of the West Country. He had begged the family to come the following week, so a pleasure trip was to be arranged. Captain Parker took his leave and on being shown out passed a gentleman on his way to pay a morning call. It was the young lawyer, Mr. Rose. Parker bowed, but could scarcely contain his irritation. His scheme was progressing well, and he cared for no obstacles to block his path. Falling back on his naval training, he muttered to himself: 'Don't give up the ship, Parker. He who has planted will preserve.'

Mrs. Austen had no desire to be thought a *catch-match maker*. Nevertheless, she regarded the visit as a great success.

'Well, my dear girls,' said she, with a teasing smile, 'now that Captain Parker has departed, I must ask – how do you find him? He certainly seems a gentleman of wit and spirit, does he not? And such attentions! I must admit, I am curious to know which of you has caught his eye.'

'Yes, Mama,' replied Jane. 'He has been … most attentive, though I believe Captain Parker's charm is such that it is difficult to discern where it is truly directed. What think you, Cassie?'

'Indeed, he is very … engaging. But I suspect he flirts with all ladies in the same manner, as he seems to take great delight in it.'

'Yes, I do not imagine he would have any preference for either of us, beyond the novelty of our conversation or our company. He is a man of good humour, and I think that is enough for him.'

Mildly crestfallen, Mrs. Austen looked from one daughter to the other. 'Well, I do not know … But you must allow, he does seem very taken with you both. I wonder which of you he will call upon again first.'

Jane shook her head. 'I daresay Captain Parker has no intention of choosing between us. His flirtations, it seems, are meant to be distributed equally. I cannot imagine his affections being anything but as transient as a passing breeze. I would hazard that tomorrow he may turn his attention elsewhere.'

Gazing out of the window, Cassie nodded her agreement. 'I think the captain's heart may be fixed on matters far beyond our reach, Mama.'

Mrs. Austen sighed. She knew that Cassie's heart was devoted to the man she had loved and lost, but she felt it her duty to inform her younger daughter that time was of the essence.

'You must be sensible, Jane, my dear, that you are not very young. You have to consider very calmly whether you would be contented to find yourself at fifty an old maid like Sophy Johnson on a scanty income, which would scarcely afford you a bone of mutton and potatoes.'

Jane responded tartly that she had never yet seen a gentleman worthy of her affection. And yet, for all her protestations, she had been impressed not only by Captain Parker's affection for her brother, but also by his powers of observation and the liveliness of his discourse.

Mr. Rose fixed his eyes on a green parasol heading up the beach, advancing briskly. Miss Jane had been dipped early that Thursday morning and was returning for her warming dish of chocolate. She was without her veil and as she approached, he observed her quick and bright eyes and the way she had of turning them swiftly on an object and holding them there. Her eyebrows, like musical slurs, were a shade darker than her hair. Her face was utterly captivating, with a frankness of expression he had not seen before in a woman.

He held out the morning paper and bade her to give it to her father with his compliments. She could not refuse his civility and, accepting, took her leave. Such impertinence! was her initial thought. Yet she could not fail to notice the elegance of his person and the sweetness of the smile he had bestowed upon her when she had accepted his offering to her father. He truly was provokingly handsome, his eyes as cerulean as the sea beyond. When he had paid his morning call yesterday, her parents had been impressed by his graceful mien and his kind consideration of trusting that the Misses Austen had not been too fatigued by the dancing.

'My Jenny is vitality itself,' her father had replied. 'Indeed, she intends to rise early on the morrow to be dipped in the ocean.' Jane had shot her father a reproving glance. She did not care to share her sea-bathing plans with a stranger. And now, this … this *lawyer* had taken advantage (there was no other expression) of her father's intelligence and had set out to discompose and cause embarrassment. She was also mortifyingly aware that she was wearing her old brown cambric gown, that her petticoat was drenched by the sea and her pink shoes sand-soiled. Her straw bonnet strings were untied and flapping furiously in the salty sea breeze. It was too agitating for him to catch her in so unguarded a manner and she had no patience with herself or him.

Once again, he looked amused and made his elegant bow, after which she bobbed and almost ran to Dove Lane. She threw her bonnet and the newspaper onto the chaise and kicked off her damp slippers. Cassie was at her easel, a crumpled ball of paper beside her, but was her usual calm and reassuring self, rising momentarily to rub her sister's feet with a napkin. 'The first thing we do, let's kill all the lawyers,' Jane intoned with a groan.

'But why have you taken such an instant dislike to the poor creature?' Cassie said reprovingly, though in her customary gentle tone.

'Saves time,' Jane retorted.

'He is just what a young man ought to be,' said Cassie. 'Sensible, good-humoured and lively. And remarkably handsome.'

'You never see a fault in anyone, all the world is agreeable in your eyes.'

'I speak what I think, but I would never wish to be hasty in censuring anybody.'

Jane glanced at her sister's easel. Cassie was putting the finishing touches to a half-length of Frank in his captain's uniform. There was no want of likeness; she had captured his intensity and vigour, and produced a charming sail ship in the background. With every effort, Cassie improved. The style was so spirited. The expression of the eye so correct. It was a rebuke to take more labours with her own endeavours.

Jane entered her bedchamber and began to set the toilet stand to rights, gathering stray garments hanging on the backs of chairs. She changed her cambric for a more comfortable and commodious wrapper and rearranged her coil of long hair, combing it with unusual energy. Sea bathing was tiring, and she felt quite vexed and out of sorts. She remembered the invitation for the family to tour the grounds of Reverend Swete's seat, Oxton. She was also soothed by thoughts of the arrival of her bosom friend, Martha Lloyd, who was to join the family in Dove Lane within the fortnight. Martha was the person with whom she shared her most intimate thoughts. She alone, outside the family circle, knew of Jane's desire to be a published author and had been privy to the intimate readings of her novels. Martha had encouraged Jane, laughed at all the right places and longed to hear more about the adventures of her intrepid heroines.

Though Jane loved her sister, the death from yellow fever of Tom Fowle, whose poor body had been cast into the sea, had placed an imperceptible barrier between them. How could she comprehend Cassie's loss? And not even a grave to visit. Her sister's fortitude was admirable, perhaps too much so, she wondered privately. If she were ever to truly love, which she very much doubted, she would be incapable of showing composure in the face of the death of a betrothed. Cassie was convinced that she could never love again, that first love was immutable. Well, that was no creed of *hers*, and a romantic notion that Jane scorned. With all her heart.

In the small hours of a hot and humid Friday night, she awoke from a nightmare in which she was standing in the park of Scarlets with her aunt. She knew it was Scarlets because she could see the large white mansion house with its twin rounded towers. Then she found herself in the wood walk of Steventon, winding through clumps of underwood, overhung by elm trees. She could see the well between the vicarage and the wood walk, and then the cucumber garden, the strawberry beds and her mother's pot herbs, marigolds and the weathercock surmounting the white pole.

The next morning, she relayed her dream to Cassie, with the admission that all dreams were dull as ditchwater for the listener.

'We all of us miss our home, my dearest Jane,' said Cassie softly. 'But we will soon take possession of another, and with our plate, linen, books and china, we shall be content.' She omitted any mention of Jane's pianoforte, which had been sold, and her father's library bequeathed to James.

'But we are now degraded to the condition of visitors,' replied Jane sharply. Seeing her sister's dismay at the violence of her emotion, she began to sing a ditty, drumming her fingers on the table as if playing a piano:

'Mistress Mary, Quite contrary,
How does your garden grow?
With Silver bells, and Cockle shells,
Sing Cuckoos all in a row.'

Jane's feelings of animosity towards her brother's second wife, once her bosom friend, had increased following the latter's ill treatment of her niece, Anna. After James's first wife had died when Anna was just two, she had been sent to Steventon to be consoled by her aunts, who raised her with all the love and concern due a motherless child. The sisters, close companions to Mary and her sister, Martha, had been only too delighted when their brother proposed to their friend, but Mary's indifference to her stepdaughter, and her vulgar delight in becoming mistress of Steventon, had cooled the friendship. It was Jane's opinion that Mary had persuaded James to expedite her father's retirement. She could not forgive her.

Cassie turned the distressing talk to their aunt Perrot and Scarlets, which as well as inheriting Steventon, James was heir to, along with a vast fortune, courtesy of their aunt and uncle.

'Frank and Charles must make their own way in the world, seek their own fortune, while James and Edward are lords of the manor,' said Jane, in no mood to be conciliatory.

'Hush, dear. Surely the good fortune of one in the family is the fortune of all?'

'Perhaps. That remains to be seen.'

With this, she terminated the conversation, fearful of losing even a precious minute more of the early morning, while the household slept, which was the time she gave to her scribbling. To return to the adventures of Elinor and Marianne, and Elizabeth and Jane, was the greatest of all pleasures. That both sets of sisters faced the turmoil of being turned out of their family home did not occur to her, and there was no reason why it should; after all, there was nothing unusual in such an event.

Leah was playing close to the water's edge, scooping up the wet sand and letting it trickle through her fingers. It was Saturday, so there were no lessons that morning. Her father watched her closely, fearing real or imaginary harm. The child was his prized pearl, six years of age, with dark curly hair and limpid green-brown eyes, and belonged to him completely, irrevocably. He would never let anyone take her from him. Until he had held her in his arms, William had not known love – now he had brought her to England to be educated and to meet her English family. He required only a propitious moment to make the relevant introductions and another to assuage the self-righteous indignation with which his mother would certainly greet the unwanted arrival. For the time being the precious child was lodged safely with her governess in the boarding house. Close to the sea, where she felt at home. She would begin to speak again soon. It was excessive shyness that was the cause, and the loss of her mother.

The mild weather would help to accustom her to the harsh English climate, and once the awkward matter of his mother's attitude was resolved she would be removed to Oxton. William's plan was meticulous and water-tight. His parents had welcomed his renunciation of his errant ways since leaving Antigua. They did not know, however, that it was entirely due to him becoming a father, and not to his moral reformation or a belated sense of filial duty. Leah was a Miss Swete. It was merely a matter of time before she took her rightful place.

In the distance, he saw a gentleman, elegantly dressed, heading across the Mall towards the circulating library. William scooped up his daughter and entrusted her to the waiting arms of her governess, Miss Sharpe. It was essential not to be seen with the girl until the time was ripe. 'Let her play a little longer,' he instructed Miss Sharpe, 'and then ensure she has a rest.' He would take his morning coffee at the Yorke. Best to avoid the London, where there were far too many of his mother's neighbourhood spies.

At the far west end of the sands, Jane was feeling refreshed by her early morning walk, accompanied by Frank and Captain Parker, who was describing the upper gun deck apartments of Admiral Nelson, decorated with a fine portrait of Lady Hamilton and depictions of the Battle of the Nile. The sea air had stirred her appetite and she was looking forward to breakfast.

Yes, Parker concurred with Frank, there was indeed a striking resemblance between Miss Jane and Emma Hamilton. The shape and brilliance of the eyes, the dark hair that curled round the face, the well-formed mouth with its cupid bow. Truly, Frank had not exaggerated his sister's beauty. Jane blushed and laughed, putting it down to a brother's fondness.

She changed the subject, begging for more details of their wooden world. Was it true that sailors captured deck rats by impaling them with their swords and cooking them over the fire to eat? What of the sailors flogged for insubordination or worse? And of mast heading, the punishment for midshipmen – entreated to climb the top mast and stay put in the freezing cold wind until permission was granted to descend? What a dreadful ordeal for a young boy! Captain Parker gave a well-bred shudder, but did not deny the rumours.

Frank noticed the little girl splashing in the shallows further down the beach. She reminded him of the children for whom he used to fashion wooden toys in his spare time and sparked a yearning in him for the East, for the white sun-drenched sands and the turquoise waters. Despite the temperate English weather, she would feel chilly, he suspected. But what was she doing here? Who were her people? With the keen eyesight of a sailor, he had spotted, from afar, the gentleman who had scurried away, and resolved to make the relevant enquiries, wishing to know more of the child. After all, it was impossible to keep secrets in a small town such as Sidmouth.

WEEK TWO

Improvement too, the idol of the age,
Is fed with many a victim. Lo, he comes!
Th' omnipotent magician, Brown, appears!
And waves his wand, and lo! the landscape bows.

(William Cowper)

The grounds of Oxton had been declared to be highly beautiful, crowned by an impressive expanse of water. Reverend Swete had promised cold provisions, and everything was to be conducted in the style of a complete party of pleasure, with open carriages to transport them; Jane hoped to sit alongside Captain Parker on the barouche-box. He arrived soon after breakfast and she was conveyed to her desired seat, glad to have an unparalleled view of the country.

Oxton House was a large, handsome stone building, standing well on rising ground and backed by a ridge of high woody hills. When issuing the invitation, the reverend had explained that upon acceding to the estate he had taken down the old mansion house and rebuilt in the Palladian style, having secured the services of Capability Brown for the landscaping. The old garden had been cleared and in its place the ingenious Brown and his industrious men had created a lawn which opened up the valley with its views over the River Exe. Various trees of ash, oak, elm, lime and sycamore had been planted in the style of the picturesque, and a curving serpentine lake created. He was most eager for them to admire his improvements.

'A fine Monday morning, Captain Parker, Miss Jane, welcome, welcome,' said Swete as he assisted her down from her seat, before turning to attend Mrs. Austen from her place within the carriage. 'We expect the others any moment. Is not that the sound of eager hooves on gravel?' He turned to the principal building. 'I flatter myself that those who can recall to their minds the state of the former mansion and its environs, will not consider the sums which I have laid out in the erection of the present house, and in the embellishment of the grounds, to have been fruitlessly expended.'

The party nodded their agreement and made all the appropriate noises.

'The magical influence of Mr. Capability Brown has enabled us to escape from the darkness of prejudice and trace the path of nature without the aid of geometric art: is not that so, Miss Jane?' the reverend continued. 'And being enabled to do so by the munificence of my ever to be honoured relation and benefactress …'

With a deep sigh of appreciation, Swete turned to look right of the house to contemplate that other requirement of the improver: 'The grandeur and the gloom of a grove of stately oaks inspire the meditating mind with sentiments of awe and veneration. If I had been a mythologist, I should most assuredly have exclaimed with the poet – *habitarant dii quoque sylvas* – *the gods have dwelt in the woods* – is that not so, Mrs. Austen?'

When the business of arriving was over, the party went inside to the drawing room to be formally welcomed by the mistress of the house and thence to an adjoining dining parlour where a collation had been prepared.

Mrs. John Swete, daughter of Lord Montague Beaumont of Combe in Gittisham, had disobliged her family by marrying a mere clergyman. She had disappointed herself by having to dispose of her visiting cards in the name of Lady Amelia Beaumont. The family had consoled themselves in the knowledge that, though the son of a surgeon by the name of Tripe, her husband's good fortune had been to inherit the commodious Oxton House and its estate: on condition that he changed his name to Swete.

Before they could consider the particular object of the day, that of taking a survey of the grounds, another visitor was announced, and in walked Samuel Rose, apologising for his lateness. Jane whispered to her sister: 'What is he doing here? He's worse than the plagues of Egypt.'

'Welcome back to Oxton, Mr. Rose,' said John Swete. 'I could not resist inviting you for a return visit, since you have shown yourself such a firm favourite with our young ones.'

To Jane's astonishment, at that moment two sturdy little fellows of four and five came racing through the door and threw themselves upon Rose, begging him to show them how to box bareknuckle like Gentleman Jackson.

'My dear sir,' said Jane to Swete, 'are these your grandchildren?'

'Good heavens no, Miss Jane – they are the youngest of my own brood of twelve chickens.'

Rose, meanwhile, was on all fours, bearing one boy on his back as another whipped him round the room as if he were a thoroughbred at the chase. Jane tried not to laugh.

Interrupting the merriment, their host suggested they take the tour of the gardens before the heat of the afternoon, so the party descended through an outward door leading to the shrubbery and grounds beyond. Attracted by plants and peacocks, they dispersed in happy independence, Captain Parker the first to move forward towards the plantations behind the house, with Jane forming a natural union, and Cassie behind with Frank and Mr. Rose.

Mrs. Austen made a slower pace with Amelia Swete and the reverend, the former making a complaint that it was already insufferably hot, and fanning herself furiously to make her point stronger. Really it was unusually warm for May – barely a breeze – better than a wet day in November – pity about her wool spencer – summer already – warmth more agreeable than cold – a lonely cloud towards the east – a little shelter under the large cedar of Lebanon – refreshments delightful – much obliged to you – such a nice party. She had given birth to eight children and grown stout, but she was still a fine-looking woman, with the small, shrewd eyes of an elephant.

Presently, they came upon a secluded spot and Reverend Swete announced with a flourish his pride and joy, the Cottage – a summer house boasting magnificent views of the valley and sea below. Built on the edge of a field high above Oxton, under a clump of ash trees, the house was large, and elegant, with a cove ceiling and three box-windows with painted glass, and a chimney piece made of marble.

Much to Mrs. Austen's relief, the Cottage's house-keeper – an elderly woman who slept in a bedroom under the stairs, according to the reverend – had provided refreshments: lemonade, ices and lavish bowls of gleaming blood-red cherries. Fatigued by the walk, the party was gratified by the opportunity to rest in the shade.

They had barely had a chance to pit the cherries before their ardent host was hurrying them on. The Cottage was not the only folly executed by Mr. Capability Brown. At the Reverend Swete's request, he had put up an abbey gateway or a 'ruin' in the wild part of the grounds, a large structure consisting of two arches in the Gothic style, peeping from amid the gloom of high rocks and venerable trees, casting its monastic reflection in the water.

'Daughters of Eve,' Swete said, turning to the young ladies with a bow, 'behold my dear old Gateway *just* what we meet with in ancient castles or abbeys' – this though it had not been erected more than two or three years before. 'It has the appearance of a ruin, and a ruin it hath literally been three times,' said he, 'for so often has it fallen due to the obstinacy, conceit and ignorance of the workmen. It has just cost me three hundred and fifty pounds to put my ruins in thorough repair. But I am content with the final result.'

Jane could not resist. 'Sir, should not the straight line of the arch be broken?'

'Or perhaps there should be an added gleam on the water under the trees, or a fake spire against the tree to terminate the prospect?'

Jane found herself laughing at Mr. Rose's intervention. Captain Parker, affronted, made his own gallant remark:

'We are in the garden of Eden, you know; in all the region of perpetual spring, youth and beauty.'

Jane's eyes met her sister's and they acknowledged the compliment with the required bob. Flattered, and seizing his opportunity, the naval man kept going, 'A most excellent serpentine! It forms a perfect maze, and winds like a true lover's knot.'

By now they had reached the latest improvement, named the Hermitage and built on a prominent position, intended as a rustic seat, where, according to the reverend, one might sit at leisure and reflect upon the diversified beauties of the surrounding scenery. Jane took a seat, finding herself beside Mr. Rose and glad of his companionable silence. After a while, he broke the spell with an expression of sorrow for having invaded her solitude that morning on the beach when she had been sea bathing.

'It wasn't of the least consequence,' said she, repressing her true feelings.

'They are indeed *very fine ruins*,' he continued with a smile, revealing even, white teeth. Provoking though he was, she arched her fine eyebrow and smiled in return, her cheeks dimpling. She took out her brisé ivory fan, with its narrow brown velvet ribbon. It was engraved with a depiction of the Battle of the Nile, which did not escape Rose's notice. Nor Captain Parker's.

The latter squeezed onto the bench and began a story of his exploits aboard the *Goliath*, a subject, to be sure, of which she could never tire. As ever, Parker was full of praise for Frank, his daring, courage and ingenuity. The time, last August, on the *Peterel*, when Captain Austen had outsmarted the French by rowing to the Turkish vessel they had secured and boldly rescuing fourteen men before setting fire to it. His success at Cádiz. Again Nelson's description of Frank as a fine sailor. This too she could listen to without end.

Catching her brother's eye, she felt gratified by his look of approbation and fondness. She wanted to please him above everything. After all, it might be something to be a sailor's wife. If she felt Mr. Rose's swift change of mood, and noticed the dark blush staining his cheek as he looked in disbelief at Captain Parker, it did not signify. He was nothing to her.

Jane rose from the seat. The rest of the party had caught up and were admiring the view. Mrs. Swete eyed her with suspicion. She did not care for this young lady, with her expression of amused scepticism. Nor was she pleased with the marked attention shown to her by the young gentlemen. She had observed Jane's coolness towards her favourite, Mr. Rose, and resented it.

'You are not fond of the picturesque, Miss Jane?' she barked. 'It is an acquired taste, but not perhaps one that will trouble you in your cosy lodgings in Sydney Place?'

'You do me wrong, madam,' replied Jane. 'I am extremely enamoured of Mr. Gilpin and have been since a young girl. A mallet judiciously used might render the insufficiently ruinous gable of Tintern Abbey more picturesque. Was not that one of his instructions?'

She continued in the same vein: 'Does he not say, also, that when it comes to a portrait, the highest form of picturesque beauty is not the "lovely face of youth smiling with all its sweet dimpling charms", but the "patriarchal head" with its lines of wisdom and experience … what is it now, ah, yes, the *rough* edges of age?'

Mrs. John Swete turned away in disgust, waving her fan furiously, but her husband, who had been surveying the sweet countryside, was roused by the mention of

Gilpin: 'Ah. Let us recall the lovely lines of Mr. Gilpin on the sea gull, best viewed not in the clear sky, but amid dark clouds. What is it now? *If the Seagull wheeling along the storm should turn its silvery side strong illumined against the bosom of some lurid cloud, by this single touch of opposition it gives double darkness to the Tempest.* Now is not that fine, Miss Jane?'

'We have certainly had ample picturesque finery during your tour today, sir. Some might say a surfeit – suitable for stronger stomachs than my own.'

The reverend looked crestfallen and hastened to summon the carriages.

As they walked back, Mr. Rose quietly took Jane aside. 'Your reflections do justice to your impeccable taste, madam. But it was perhaps a trifle unkind to speak thus to our enthusiastic host.'

Jane said nothing. However, in the carriage on the way back to Sidmouth, she was overcome with contrary sentiments. How dare Mr. Rose upbraid her in such a manner? She had spoken but in jest – and yet ... was he not perhaps correct that her words to the well-intentioned reverend had been lacking in tact? Mr. Rose may be a gentleman to be reckoned with. She had not before encountered a man so ready to speak his mind as was she her own.

'Your first position is false, my dear sister. Mr. Rose and Captain Parker are not well acquainted. There is no mystery.'

'My eyes did not deceive me, nor did my reason,' Jane replied firmly. 'Some prior connection is evident.'

'Do not be so sure, dear sister. May their rivalry not pertain to some future connection?'

Jane did not reply. She walked to her writing box and took out the letter she had promised to read to Cassie. 'Hastings has been breeched, Henry has quarrelled with his tailor and Eliza has a new slouch bonnet. And *that* is all the news from Hans Place.'

Jane wondered if she should wear white gloves or blue with her yellow and white cloud gown for the Tuesday morning walk to Peak Hill with Captain Parker and Frank. She would wear her new chip hat trimmed with white ribbon. Or should she rely on her straw bonnet to shield her skin from the sun?

'Do remember to tie your bonnet strings,' Cassie begged. 'It will be blustery on the hill.'

'A southwesterly, to be precise,' said Frank, coming through the open door into the drawing room. He cocked his head to one side and reviewed his sister critically. 'I prefer the white Indian muslin with the short sleeves.'

She tapped him on the shoulder with her fan. 'I shall wear my light lace cloak, just to please you.'

'Did I hear you discuss Captain Parker and Mr. Rose? I can assure you there is no "prior connection", as you put it. Their paths have never crossed. I should know it if they had. Mr. Rose is a fine fellow, is he not? I hear he is a friend of the abolitionists.'

'He is a most disagreeable man who has an irksome habit of appearing unexpectedly and without invitation,' Jane retorted, remembering her embarrassment at the bathing machines. 'A man of uncertain taste, too, considering his interest in boxing. I detest him and all his works.'

'Why will you delight in making yourself appear worse than you are, my dear?' said Cassie.

'Because I hate to be like other people,' said Jane, laughing, as the maid opened the drawing room door and in walked Captain Parker. 'How happy I am to see you, Captain Parker,' said Jane, bundling a sheaf of papers from the table into her writing box.

'Jane's had a busy morning,' Frank said by way of explanation when the morning greetings were over. 'She composes novels that are almost as perfect as the letters she writes to me at sea. We have been delighted with the adventures of Jane and Elizabeth, but which is the heroine? I rather suppose the younger sister?'

'In my novels, all of the most beautiful women shall be called Jane,' said she with an arch glance at Cassie.

Captain Parker confirmed that he was a reader of novels and a patron of his ship's well-stocked library. But a thought struck him forcefully that it would be prudent to take extra care so he said nothing more on the subject, and the trio left Dove Lane, with Parker complimenting Miss Jane on her choice of gown and sturdy walking shoes.

Once they reached the summit of Peak Hill, they fell silent as they watched the flowing of the tide. Jane turned her gaze on Frank who was scanning the horizon, deep in thought. Was he thinking of Naples or Gibraltar? Battles lost or won? Gulls circled overhead screeching, in a sky the delicate blue-green of a robin's egg, slowly hardening to azure. The fishing boats creaked and groaned, the sea sparkling in the early morning sunlight. Under the cliffs, patches of green gardens strewn with washing lines of snow-white linen fluttered in the breeze. A lonely sailboat, full-bellied, glided westwards.

Jane risked a glance at Captain Parker through the interstices of her straw bonnet. His face in profile was striking. He too was lost in rumination as he surveyed the ocean. She felt a rush of sadness, perhaps hopelessness from him, which she could not explain or account for; only that it was as indubitable as the nose on her face. Then with a cheery smile he turned to her and made mention of the dolphins to be seen playing in the shallows, their backs glistening, and a cormorant dipping for

eels or water snakes. For just a moment, to be joined
with these two fine sailors, to be part of their enviable
world, appeared to her to be the greatest possible happiness. She could think of no other.

The drawing room at Oxton House was a chamber of
severe elegance, its lofty windows affording a fine view
of the garden, but its atmosphere was, on this occasion,
oppressively heavy. Mrs. Swete, her formidable figure
stiffly erect in an armchair upholstered in sage-green
damask, gazed upon her son with an expression of
mingled disdain and incredulity. The Reverend Mr.
Swete, seated by the fire with his hand resting on his
walking stick, appeared more pensive than angry, though
his countenance betrayed a degree of concern.

Their firstborn William stood before them with an air
of resolute calm, looking slightly flushed from the exertions of his earlier play on the beach. The child in
question was, mercifully, not present, having been left in
the care of her governess at their lodgings. Yet her
shadow hung heavily over the room, as though her small
figure occupied every corner of it.

'Well, William,' began Mrs. Swete, her voice sharp,
imperious, 'we are waiting. Who, pray, is this child with

whom you have seen fit to make a public spectacle of yourself upon the sands? Do not think to prevaricate, for the truth is already half-exposed.'

William's jaw tightened, but he remained composed. 'The child, madam, is my daughter.'

'Your *what*?' Mrs. Swete's voice rose to a pitch of incredulity, her usually pale features acquiring a mottled hue. 'You dare to claim her as your daughter? And what, pray, is the mother's name? Some woman of Antigua, no doubt – a creature of no breeding, no refinement, and, I presume, no lawful connection to yourself.'

'Maria was a woman of Antigua, it is true,' replied William steadily, 'and a slave, as were her parents before her. She bore me a daughter, and in doing so she gave me new life. My Leah is now all that remains of her mother, and I have resolved to give her a place in the world befitting her innocence and worth.'

'A slave's child? You would bring such a stain upon the Swete name – upon *my* name? The daughter of a creature scarcely human?'

'Amelia,' interjected the Reverend Swete in a mild but firm tone, 'let us not descend into such language. The child is here, and she is innocent. Whatever may be the circumstances of her birth, she cannot be held accountable for them.'

Mrs. Swete turned upon her husband with a look of astonishment. 'John, you cannot mean to condone this! A bastard child of the colonies, brought to England, introduced into society under our name? I shall not endure it!'

'I am not asking you to endure anything, madam,' said William, his voice rising slightly but still controlled. 'I ask only that you do not condemn an innocent child for the sins of her father, if sins they must be called. She is my daughter, and I love her. If that is an offence, then let it be mine alone.'

The Reverend Swete leaned back in his chair, his brow furrowed. At last he said, 'William, you have erred, but you have also shown a strength of character in seeking to make amends. The child, whatever her parentage, is part of our family, and I shall not turn her away.'

'John!' Mrs. Swete exclaimed, her voice trembling with outrage. 'You cannot be serious! This affront – this humiliation – it will be the ruin of us!'

'I think not,' replied her husband quietly. 'I think it is, rather, an opportunity for us to show Christian charity.'

Mrs. Swete rose abruptly, her lace cap trembling with the violence of her indignation. 'Christian charity? This is more than I can bear. You may do as you please, John, but I shall not stay to witness it and that child will not enter this house while I am the mistress of it.'

She swept from the room, her skirts rustling with righteous fury, and did not stop until she reached her bedchamber, where she declared herself indisposed and would stay for the rest of the day.

William, though shaken, turned to his father with gratitude in his eyes. 'Thank you, sir. I feared I would find no ally here.'

The reverend sighed heavily. 'Your mother will come round in time, I hope. But, William, take care – this path you have chosen is not without its trials. You must be prepared to face them, for your sake and hers.'

'I am prepared,' said William firmly. 'For her, I would face the world.'

And with that, the father and son sat in silence, the weight of the moment pressing upon them both.

After the cliff walk, Parker proposed another expedition, this time to Shaldon to see the famous Amazonian Sirens, so within two days they were out together again. To avoid the evil of interlopers, the captain had suggested the party be confined to at most a snug half-dozen. Since Mrs. Austen was in bed with a cold, and therefore staying at home with her husband, in her place he had suggested Mrs. Honeychurch, proprietress of the circulating library, could act as chaperone. This sensible, genteel woman who had befriended Miss Jane and the family, as patrons of the circulating library and being so fond of novels, had agreed. It would be a pleasure to accompany the young ladies, and the two captains, she said. Her eldest daughter could take care of the library in her absence, so Sidmouth would not suffer without her.

They had a very fine day for the visit and after a long drive to Teignmouth, they awaited the ferry to carry them over to the village of Shaldon – to be conveyed by the celebrated women rowers, whose menfolk fished in Newfoundland all summer, leaving them to provide for their families. As well as ferrying people and provisions back and forth, often in dangerous weather, the women fished for oysters and salmon.

'How do you do? exclaimed a familiar voice with delight at seeing the young people. It was the Reverend Swete on his donkey. 'Another glorious morning, and I see you feasting your eyes on our rowers – you will see how the female inhabitants of this salutary and *piscaine* shore, from being accustomed to draw their subsistence in nets from the bosom of the ocean, have acquired all that firmness of tone in their bodies and that intrepidity of mind peculiar to the sons of Neptune (with a bow to the captains) – shooting their seams, rowing and navigating their boats with as much dexterity and spirit as any British tars.'

The reverend was in full flight again, turning serious to regale the party with a disaster that had recently befallen the Shaldon women, in which three of four sisters had perished while supplying a privateer, the *Bellona*, with a cargo of smuggled spirits, an event he had borne witness to. A strong gust of wind had capsized the ship and it had sunk perpendicular to the bottom of the ocean.

'I was sat at table in full view of her and was admiring her beauty, and with what velocity she flew through the waters, when in an instant, she was struck, her port holes filled with water, and down she went. I never felt as at that moment in my life – I even now shudder in the relation, *infandum piaget renovare dolorem!* … the piercing cries of the people on the shore, who lamented a father, husband, sister or brother were almost beyond conception, distressful. Only one half was saved, the others being in a state of intoxication between the decks – miserably perished – and only one sister rescued. Now I am done with this melancholy tale. Good day to you.'

He trotted away on Joseph, his satchel and paints slung over his back, leaving Jane to muse on the sisters who had lost their lives and the one that had survived and been left behind. How could she bear such a loss?

As the ferry approached, the party observed the strapping Sapphos up close, bronzed and muscular, dressed in britches, naked from feet to knees, and wearing straw bonnets of uncouth shapes tied on their heads. Captain Parker was the first to speak. 'I must admit, Miss Jane, I had not anticipated such a sight upon my arrival at the ferry. These women – so strong and sure of their course – put me in mind of the boldest mariners I have ever encountered. What a contrast they present to the delicate creatures of society.'

'Indeed, Captain,' she replied, with a laugh, 'I confess, the notion of a woman wielding an oar with such vigour does somewhat o'erturn the usual expectations of femininity. One might almost be led to think them the very picture of a *sea captain* rather than the good wives of a Devonshire village.'

'You are not wrong, Miss Jane. One might even fancy that these ladies, rather than tending to the dainty arts of embroidery and pianoforte, might be better suited to navigating the very seas themselves. I imagine they could give any British tar a run for his money.'

'Oh, I am sure of it. If it were not for their, shall we say, *unconventional* manner of dress, one might suppose them some sort of naval officers in disguise. Such independence of spirit! They are, assuredly, women of the most engaging fortitude and temper – qualities not always appreciated in our own sex, I fear.'

'So you are not averse to the idea of women showing themselves as capable as men – perhaps even in matters of the heart as much as the oar?'

'Captain, I believe that women are as prone to folly as men, and as capable of serious judgement when the occasion demands it. As for these Sapphos, I have no doubt their hearts and hands are equally steadfast, though perhaps with less concern for the propriety of their demeanour than might be deemed fitting in polite society.'

'And perhaps, Miss Jane, that is just what makes them worthy of admiration. After all, is it not the bold and the strong who ought to command our respect, regardless of whether they sit at the bow or the stern?'

With this flourish, he handed the three women into the first boat. Mrs. Honeychurch, who had been discomposed by the talk of Sapphos, was glad the conversation, lacking in the necessary degree of propriety, had come to an end. She asked nervously if the weather was set fair. Parker assured her that indeed it was, but Jane noticed a shadow flicker across Frank's face as he surveyed the horizon.

The sea was as smooth as glass on the short crossing to Shaldon, a pretty seaside village of tightly packed fishermen's cottages along narrow streets and winding back lanes, surrounded by rolling hills. On seeing the heavy fishing nets laid out to dry, Jane wondered how many women it would take to cast them.

'Why, this is just the place for retired admirals and captains,' said Frank. 'Close as it is to the sea and its three fine shipyards.'

Captain Parker, energised by the sight of the yards and the Shaldon Sapphos, was of a sudden in high spirits. He drew Jane to one side and whispered a remark that caused her colour to rise. As Cassie and Frank came near, the captain clapped his hand on his friend's shoulder.

'How much I am obliged to you,' said he, 'for telling me to come to Sidmouth! If it had not been for you, I should certainly have lost all the happiness of the party. There is such sweetness in the air of Devon; its beauty and effect not perhaps to be found rivalled.'

'I was a kinder friend than you deserved,' replied Frank, with a fond smile. 'Though I long wanted you to make the acquaintance of my sisters. On the *Lark*, I remember your interest in the letter case I carved for Jane.'

'And so exquisite a carving, if I may be so bold, sir? A worthy offering to a devoted correspondent. If only I had a sister to write to me at sea and care whether or not I ended at the bottom of the ocean. And I trust (from the discerning reflections of the good ladies) that your own epistles proved to be a reliable guide to all naval matters. My poor mother could hardly believe we used knives and forks, had servants to attend us, and cooks to furnish our meat with sauces.'

'Frank's letters were indeed detailed, and never too long,' said Jane, with a playful expression. 'And you were a kind and exacting commander – fastidious, too, with keeping the sloop *ship shape*.'

'Ah! I see my faithful friend has tittle-tattled. Thirty lashes of the cat, for you, Captain Austen. You are referring, no doubt, to my mosquito quiz, Miss Jane? I left two mosquitoes squished on the wall above my hammock and waited to see if they were removed and the walls scrubbed clean on my return. You may be amused, Miss Jane, but the wretched things are no laughing matter in the Indies. Lost many a good fellow to Yellow Jack, and tossed him into Davy Jones's Locker. The devil is in the details.'

Only Jane observed the shudder with which Cassie turned away, wrapping her lace shawl closely around her shoulders. The captain must have been ignorant, or had perhaps forgotten the circumstances of Tom Fowle's death. He was not to blame. It was she who was at fault and her mortification at causing such unhappiness to a beloved sister was immense. How could she have encouraged his prattle and betrayed Frank's confidence?

By the time they advanced to the return ferry, the breeze had increased, whipping the waves and making Jane's untied bonnet ribbons flap and dance. Mrs. Honeychurch glanced anxiously towards the gathering clouds. As they walked, Jane and Captain Parker exchanged a look. He found the frankness of her expression captivating and though not an 'apple cleft in two', the resemblance between sister and brother was arresting. In character, they were dissimilar. The brother so reserved and the sister so spirited. Yet Parker was drawn to Frank's diffident, principled nature precisely *because* it was so different to his own. His friend was incapable of dissimulation.

Jane observed with gratitude the loving glance Parker bestowed on her brother. 'Your affection for Frank does you much credit, Captain. A life at sea creates bonds of comradeship, *brothers in arms*, does it not? Let us disprove Dr. Johnson's claim that being in a ship is being in a gaol, with the chance of being drowned.'

'I have never felt more liberated than on board a sloop. It is no prison to me,' said he with a deep sigh. 'It is no trial to respect and esteem your brother. He's so unlike me. I could never love anyone with a disposition like my own.'

They approached the ferry via a small jetty, which creaked and groaned above the swell of water, causing Jane to look with alarm at the ever-widening gap; the boat seeming to slip away from the dock with every gust of wind. Frank took matters into his own hands, lifting Cassie into his arms and stepping across the gangplank. Jane looked at Captain Parker with a smile of assent, and he scooped her up, light as a feather, and deposited her into the ferry. 'We must not spoil those pink slippers,' said he with a laugh.

As if on cue the clouds united over their heads and a driving rain set full in their faces. The ferry rocked on the swell and a huge wave crashed over the bow. Unperturbed, the Sapphos rowed hard, muscles bulging, skirts hooked up beyond their knees as the ferryboat lurched and swayed and Cassie and Mrs. Honeychurch looked on in fear. In an instant, Captain Parker got up and seated himself beside them and started an amusing tale of an officer's parrot who repeated the ribaldry of the crew, then he pointed to the dry land and predicted that the worst of the storm was over. When the wind blew noisily, he began to sing a sea shanty in a good, strong baritone. Before long, and thus happily distracted, they reached the shoreline.

The next morning, this time accompanied by Frank, Jane kept her appointment to return to the sea to be dipped. She had erred in going alone on the morning she had met Mr. Rose and vowed to be more careful. Brother and sister were subdued. Cassie had been silent and withdrawn throughout the previous evening, though she had insisted it was fatigue from the exertions of the pleasure party and the perils of the storm, which had brought on the headache. Jane had dabbed lavender water on Cassie's temples and refrained from conversation that could only agitate.

The day was still, the sea becalmed, the morning air fresh and clear. Jane greeted Molly, entered the bathing machine and undressed into her linen smock and cap, twisting her hair into a coil. The first dip was the most bracing and she gave herself to the waves and the sharp shock of the salty sea, floating on her back while Molly held her by the arms with a practised grip. How light she felt, suspended by the gentle waves. Her thoughts drifted – to Cassie and poor Tom … and to Captain Parker and Frank – and to the morning when she had met Mr. Rose and how he had smiled at her with such warmth and sweetness of expression. She stayed in too long.

Nonetheless buoyed by the invigorating dip, she dressed and paid Molly, and sat to wait for Frank who had gone off to take another inspection of the fishing nets.

'Did not Captain Parker speak unwisely when he told of mosquitoes and yellow fever in the presence of poor Cassie?' she enquired as she took her brother's arm on his return.

'I blame myself, and myself only,' said he. 'The captain is not a careless man and thinks only of the comfort of others. I should have been sure to have made him fully sensible of Cassie's loss. Her self-command and forbearance prohibit pity, and it is not always evident how much she suffers. To those who do not know her as you do, she may appear to lack your openness and ardour of mind.'

'Her composure of temper is all to her credit. Few could endure the loss of such a man as Tom. Nor should they. And to die so far from home, and buried at sea so that she has not even a grave to visit. Do not doubt, dear Frank, the extent of her suffering. All her hopes dashed. Though, to be sure, it is no creed of mine that there is only one single and constant attachment, and that all the happiness of one's life depends upon any particular person.'

Frank looked at her with an arched expression.

'And that a *particular person*, who would appear to regard *you* in sincere admiration, has overstayed his welcome, has surely not escaped your attention. He may be recalled any minute, Jane, such a favourite as he is with the admiral. Captain Parker seeks a wife. You have spoken of your envy of the wives of sailors. Shall you be snug on board the captain's frigate?'

'As snug and cosy as you command. And I shall secure a part with the theatrical players, or, perhaps, strike some Attitudes à la Lady Hamilton.'

As they talked, they came upon a child playing in the sand, the very same one Frank had observed earlier. She was a bonny girl, with an intelligent air, but she made no sound, no utterance. Her large green-brown eyes took in everything. To his astonishment, Frank saw that she was accompanied by not only her governess but also Reverend Swete.

With a blush, the reverend greeted the pair, begging them to make the acquaintance of his granddaughter. The girl rose to her feet and executed a charming curtsy, before retiring with her governess. Momentarily lost for words, Swete soon regained his composure. Miss Swete was his son's child – her mother had died in Antigua – brought to England to be educated – she had not spoken a single word since the death of her mother – father and daughter seen together on the sands – word reached Oxton – his wife mortified – her favourite son, you see – the shock too much – taken to her bed – son banished – but hopes of a reconciliation – well, he must be off – *tempus fugit* – will be delighted to see them at the next assembly.

So the mystery was solved, thought Frank. The wild son sent to his mother's plantations in Antigua to reform his ways, bringing back a daughter of Africa. Well, he would not be the first or the last, he mused.

He noticed that Jane was enraptured by the silent girl, who was only a little more advanced in years than Anna, but the latter was a spirited child, and a prattler. Here was another motherless little girl, and yet what a world of difference between them!

Jane was the first to speak. 'My dear Frank, what can be done? In a child so young there can be no consolation for the loss of a parent. Her grandmama may *never* be reconciled to the idea. She is not a woman of liberal notions, but proud, and obstinate. She cares greatly for the distinctions of rank and is no friend to the abolition.'

'She has certainly won the heart of her grandfather,' said her brother, 'and that is a good beginning.'

'But she will be made an object of curiosity, it cannot be denied. And she is a stranger in a strange land, more likely to receive contumely than consideration. Perhaps, even, an object of aversion for those with prejudiced minds.'

'My dear Jane, there are many such children who cross the Atlantic at the behest of their doting fathers. Though his natural daughter, she will be educated as a young lady in order to qualify her to enjoy the privileges and immunities of her birthright. Think of dear Lady Brocas, our own friend and neighbour.'

Frank's reassurances belied his own fears. He thought with revulsion of the Portuguese slaver ship he had captured two years before, and the ugly scenes of human degradation and misery that had assailed him. *Soft airs and gentle heavings of the wave/Impel the fleet, whose errand is to save.*

It had not troubled *his* conscience to punish the miscreants responsible for such odious and unchristian conduct. And there, his beloved Parker and he were not in agreement; a stain on the otherwise unblemished character of his dear friend. If Jane were to discover the captain was a friend of the slave trade, she would never agree to marry him. Only Jane could reform him, of that Frank was sure. Parker was not beyond redemption – if he could be made to see the people of Africa as Frank saw them, as brothers and sisters, then there was hope. Perhaps this little girl would be the means of saving his soul, and his sister, his heart.

Jane had been busy with her own schemes for Frank's domestic happiness. Within a week Martha Lloyd would be in Sidmouth, and it was Jane's dearest wish that Frank should be settled for life with her bosom friend. Cassie was slow to share her sister's enthusiasm for the match.

'Is it not enough that one sister is wed to our brother, without wishing for another?' said she.

'Martha is a very superior being and is good enough even for such a brother as Frank. Indeed, she is too good for him, and as nobody minds having what is too good for them, then all shall be well.'

'The life of a sailor's wife is not to everyone's taste and, though Martha is robust, there is a dissimilarity of temper that may preclude her happiness. Frank is open-hearted and plain-speaking, a true sailor. Martha is a woman of sensibility, and she is dependable and amiable, but does she have the stomach for a life on board ship? Or for the anguish of uncertainty during periods of enforced separation?'

Jane eyed her sister suspiciously.

'Do we not speak at cross-purposes? Do we not consider Martha's prospects, or perhaps someone closer is in mind? And if your thoughts run on Captain Parker, I must insist that I am by no means assured of his regard for me. No absolute dependence can be given by man to any woman's declaration or intents.'

Cassie could not help laughing. 'Excuse me,' she said, 'and be assured that I meant no offence to you by speaking frankly. One advantage will proceed from this delay. *I* shall not lose you so soon.'

Jane was instantly softened. 'My dearest sister. You shall not lose me at all. I must confess that though Captain Parker is all that is amiable, there is a want of spirit about him, which if it did not denote indifference, speaks of something almost as unpromising. At times I believe his affection to be no more than friendship.'

Cassie gave her sister a quizzical look and said no more. To her, it seemed evident that the captain was deeply in love. She had observed the manner in which he searched her sister's lovely face and her fine eyes, as though desperately endeavouring to discover something elusive and equivocal. Tender as she was, his melancholic expression pulled at her heartstrings. Jane was quite wrong. She had captured his heart fully and irrevocably. Cassie knew what it felt to love and be loved, and she would do everything in her power to ensure her sister did not throw away her chance of a life of happiness. Of Martha and Frank she felt much less sanguine. Only time would tell.

Very few days passed when Captain Parker did not call at Dove Lane, leaving Cassie in a strong position to scrutinise and approve him further. Evenings at home often concluded with cards. One rainy evening late that week, before supper, Mrs. Austen, no longer complaining of indisposition, proposed a rubber of Casino. They chose their partners and were to draw their cards. Parker sat close to Jane at the card table, making his preference clear, and opposite Frank and Cassie, the latter of whom was well-placed for observation and detection. Mr. Austen, who was not fond of cards, sat out, while Mrs. Austen was dealer. Frank quickly built up his trick pile and made his first sweep. Luck was on his side.

'If I should happen to cut out,' said he, 'I may be of some use in replenishing the Madeira.'

Jane rose to help her brother, incurring the mild displeasure of the captain, ill-disposed to lose his companion.

'Perhaps you will be as well pleased not to cut in till another rubber, or will you take your chance now?'

She agreed to stay for the round and handed the keys to the wine closet to Frank. Sitting next to Parker, she noted his manly hands as he captured the cards. To her astonishment, she saw they were trembling. He requested yet another glass of Madeira, his face not flushed but pale, his eyes glassy. Frank, who had drunk only to elevate his spirits, and not to confuse his intellect, was rendered conscious of his friend's transgression in the company of the women. Yet it was discourteous to refuse and he refilled Parker's glass with the blood-red wine.

'Steady there, my good man,' said he. He had seen many a tar flogged for drunkenness, but Captain Parker was drinking glass after glass, as though his very life depended on it.

'It is devilish fine wine. Was not a bowl of wine the cause of the demise of Alexander the Great?' the captain observed, with a tired smile. 'All sorts of disreputable characters flock to the seaside, Miss Austen.'

The room fell silent. An air of gloom hung over the evening like the aroma of snuff.

'Put away the cards, girls,' said Mrs. Austen. 'We will resume yesterday's reading and we shall each read a page in turn.' Her manoeuvre to restore calm was derailed by Parker's unsuccessful attempt to rise to his feet without stumbling. Frank grabbed his arm, made his excuses for his friend and offered to escort him back to his lodgings. 'The sea air will do you good, my friend.'

'Yes, the sea air will do me good,' the captain repeated dully, then mumbled his apologies and took his leave with a clumsy bow.

Jane was thankful her father had dozed off in front of the fire. She was not at all shocked by the picture of a gentleman dead drunk, it was hardly an uncommon sight, but it occurred to her that there was something of a peculiar turn. It was the cause of much discussion when the sisters retired to undress for bed. Cassie was sure that an excess of nerves had set him off. Jane did not contradict her sister, but remained unconvinced. Was it oppression of spirits? Or something hereditary in him? She wondered, with little intermission, what could be the reason for it; was sure there must be some bad news, and thought over every kind of distress that could have befallen him.

WEEK THREE

The Mind's soft Guardian, who, tho' yet unsung,
Inspires with harmony the female tongue.

(William Hayley)

'It is a great deal too bad. What is to be done?' Mr. Samuel Rose was writing to his friend, William Hayley. Having ended his letter with such a flourish, he mopped his brow – by God it was warm – and pulled out his gold watch and chain from his pocket. Aha, it was time for the circulating library to be opened. He must be first in line, though he doubted sincerely that any other visitor would be rushing to the Shed on such a fine day. He folded the letter and sealed it with his signet ring, then gave it to his housekeeper to be delivered to Sussex. Not entirely sure Hayley has had his money's worth, he thought ruefully.

It was a glorious Monday morning, though in the distance cumulus clouds were forming. He would not be dismayed. Not with the company of a good novel and a glass of Madeira. He grabbed his gloves and hat, deciding at the last minute to forgo his umbrella. When he reached the Mall, he found it deserted, the bathers long gone for breakfast. He enjoyed the sound of the crashing of the waves on the pebbles. The sea air, as promised by Dr. Russell, was undoubtedly improving his temper and his health.

The sight of the girl by the water's edge, watched closely by her governess, directed his thoughts back to his letter and started his blood boiling again as he recalled events which had conspired against him and the cause. The treachery of Norris would never be forgotten. Initially so charming, the wretched, duplicitous man had promised to expose the horrors of the abominable trade to Parliament and then betrayed the cause at the last hour. Norris was the worst villain of them all, with no sense of his own degradation. How brazenly he claimed that the slaves had excellent, well-ventilated quarters, ate delicious food, danced and sang, and made necklaces out of African beads; were even given treats of brandy and cigarettes. Coxcomb! Rose had seen the ship's logbook that told of an insurrection which Norris had quelled with two deaths and twenty-four lashes each for the women who led it. How he had shot the ringleader with his own hands.

He must keep a cool head, he admonished himself. Cowper had done so much to galvanise the cause with his magnificent poetry. *We have no slaves at home, then why abroad?* Mr. Rose muttered aloud, to no one in particular. His mind was becalmed by the sight of the empty Shed. No doubt he would fetch his prize today, the panacea he required to quell the violence of his passion. She alone would restore him to reason and tranquillity.

He found Mrs. Honeychurch waiting with his package, which she had wrapped with paper and ribbon. She handed it to him, smiling profusely, or so he thought. She was *quite* a friend to Mr. Rose, who was not ashamed to be a novel reader. Such a fine gentleman, and so well bred. She had not seen his like in Sidmouth. He had an air of fashion and was manly, with an intelligent countenance and humour in his eyes. His complexion clear, if a little pale. A few more weeks by the sea would soon improve him. Despite being of large fortune, and good connections, he was, she heard, devoted to the law and a man of principle. He had been a friend of the poet, Mr. Cowper, she had been reliably informed. Perhaps he might make the acquaintance of her daughter? Would he be so kind as to take a look at the trinkets for sale? A brooch for Mrs. Rose? Ah, there was no Mrs. Rose.

He turned with his prize, only to discover that he was not alone. He flushed crimson on seeing that Miss Jane Austen, unchaperoned, had appeared through the library door. If he had hoped to find her confused, or disorientated, he was disappointed. She looked him in the eye, bobbed and bade him good morning. He found himself rooted to the spot, feeling unaccountably foolish. He felt rather than heard her ask in the sweetest of tones, whether Miss Edgeworth's novel had arrived. She had been waiting with great anticipation. He turned and proffered his package.

'Miss Jane, would you allow me ...'

'But what is this, Mr. Rose?'

'*Belinda*, Miss Austen.'

'Certainly not, Mr. Rose. I will not hear of it. I shall have to wait another day to discover Miss Belinda's adventures. Good day to you, sir.' She walked briskly out of the door and on to the Mall. He hurried after her, anxious not to lose ground.

'Miss Austen. I beg you.' His air of supplication was so full of warmth and humility that she could not resist. With a smile, revealing a charming dimple, she accepted the package.

'And perhaps, if it is not too much trouble, we could take a moment or two to reflect upon Miss Edgeworth's novel when we have finished reading the volumes?'

'Mr. Rose, are you always so persistent?'

'Oh, much more so. It serves me well in the courts of law.'

At the mention of his profession her face darkened. She had almost begun to forget why she disliked him so much and was grateful for the reminder.

'Miss Austen, would you give me permission to call on your father today with my newspaper?'

'You need no sanction from me, Mr. Rose. You must do as you wish. Good day to you.'

A few drops of soft summer rain had begun to fall, but before Mr. Rose could offer his umbrella, she had walked away with the same brisk, confident air that had first attracted him when he saw her on the sands with her brother. His attention was momentarily distracted as he glanced across the promenade and saw once again the little girl with the dark curly hair paddling her feet by the water's edge. He would like to know her history. He would make it his business to discover who she was and what had brought her to the Sidmouth shore so far from her native home.

Not even the rain that had continued to fall steadily could dampen Jane's spirits at the prospect of welcoming Martha to Devonshire. She rejoiced at the sight of her friend, greeting her with the liveliest pleasure. She was a dear reminder of home. They spent the morning chiefly in talking over the Hampshire news and telling again what had already been written.

Miss Lloyd was a woman below the middling height, with a round, homely face and sandy-coloured hair. She still bore the scars of a smallpox epidemic, which had taken the life of her younger brother and disfigured the face of her sister, Mary. Unlike her younger sister, Martha paid little attention to her complexion, and was a cheerful woman of sense and practicality. She physicked the local children with her home-grown remedies, nursed her ailing mother and helped Mary with the children after the marriage to James Austen. Her pockmarked face was a constant reminder to the Austen siblings of their gratitude to their Hampshire neighbour, Madam Lefroy, who had inoculated them all with her own hands. They were fortunate to have escaped the smallpox unscathed.

Martha was eager to share the news of the family, having stayed recently with Jane's brother Henry at Hans Place in London.

'How does Henry do, and Eliza, and poor little Hastings?' asked Jane. 'I hear he has been breeched now.'

'Eliza remains in excellent good looks. She returns from Sussex, having taken Hastings for the waters, and the latter is improved favourably. He begins to speak and walk just a little, and is under the care of an esteemed surgeon. Henry, as you are aware, is the most devoted of husbands and fathers.'

'Eliza's constancy and steadfastness cannot be doubted. But surely, there is little that can be done for the child?' enquired Jane.

'She is indefatigable in her care towards him and will brook no dissent as to the improvement in his condition. She convinces herself that he grows stronger every day. Her doctor recommends that he be sent away, but she will hear none of it.'

Jane blushed and thought for a moment about her own incapacitated brother, George, sent away from his mother, and his family, and taken care of and loved by his adopted parents. Yet they could be no substitute for flesh and blood relations. Perhaps it was best not to linger on the past, the remembrance of which could bring only pain. She took out a white Kashmir shawl, one of several brought by Frank from the East Indies, and placed it around her friend's slender shoulders, twirling her round to face the looking glass.

'Why, Miss Lloyd, you look so well. Allow me to make you a present of it. I have so many shawls that I shan't miss this one.' Her tone was firm and insistent, and Martha accepted it with a grateful smile.

She wished to know more of Sidmouth, of Frank and his friend Captain Parker. At that moment, the very man himself entered the parlour and with a bow made his introduction.

'Fine weather for ducks, Miss Austen. How do you do, Miss Lloyd. We shall soon have the sun shining again. There is a good southwesterly wind afoot and it shall blow away the sea mist, mark my words. What do you have there, Miss Jane?'

Parker flicked through the pages of *Belinda*. 'Not much of a novel reader, myself, much prefer poetry. "The Rime of the Ancient Mariner" – now there's a story for a seafaring man: *Water, water everywhere and not a drop to drink.*'

The captain was unfortunate in his prognosis as the rain fell steadier. He begged Miss Jane to read aloud – he had heard reports of her dramatic skills – and she took up a volume of her favourite, Cowper.

Frank came in soaked to the skin, his crop of black curly hair glistening like a seal. Captain Parker gave him an appreciative look. Frank greeted Martha warmly, and disappeared to change his clothes. Meanwhile, the remainder of the family gathered in the parlour, where a fire had been lit and a dish of chocolate prepared.

'Poor Mr. Cowper,' said Mr. Austen, with a deep sigh. '*God moves in a mysterious way, His wonders to perform.* Quite the hymn writer. And a personal favourite with *this* clergyman. Now, Jenny, what is it to be today? Something cheerful to brighten up a dull day. Do you not agree, Mrs. Austen?'

His lady did agree, though she was not at all confident that Jane would oblige. Her daughter's taste in poetry was peculiar. She herself was partial to doggerel verse, and not above penning a couplet or two, being quite a wit and a favourite among the schoolboys her husband had taught at Steventon. Her mind drifted briefly to poor dead Tom Fowle and what might have been if only Lord Craven had not dragged him to the Indies. She glanced at Cassie, the model of rectitude and delicacy, and employed in trimming a hat with pink ribbon. Perhaps Mr. Rose would do? He was good-looking and rich, and he appeared to have taken a liking to one of her daughters, given how he sent over his newspaper to Mr. Austen every morning. Jane was taken. It was evident that Captain Parker admired her and singled her out above all others. She would make a good sailor's wife. There would be no nasty surprises aboard ship.

Jane had chosen lines from *Charity*, and only the patter of the rain on the roof could be heard beating a rhythmic drum as she recited in a clear and sonorous voice:

But ah! what wish can prosper, or what prayer,
For merchants rich in cargoes of despair,
Who drive a loathsome traffic, gauge, and span,
And buy the muscles and the bones of man?
The tender ties of father, husband, friend,
All bonds of nature in that moment end.

The poem was so dear to her that she did not require the book of verse to guide her: it was imprinted on her heart. As she paused, there came a knock on the door, a voice within, and the maid announcing a visitor. A bedraggled figure appeared in a cloak from which he removed the morning's newspaper to present to Mr. Austen, who received it gratefully. Mrs. Austen was all smiles and courtesy, and begged him to take a seat by the fire.

'Pray continue, my dear child,' said Jane's father. She was embarrassed, but not to be bowed, and continued in her clear tones:

Canst thou, and honour'd with a Christian name,
Buy what is woman-born, and feel no shame?
Trade in the blood of innocence, and plead
Expedience as a warrant for the deed?

Captain Parker blushed, and Frank threw him an anxious look as Jane recited. Was this some kind of trick? Oh if so, it was a low blow. Lord Nelson himself would exclaim against this insolence, friend as he was to the *merchants*. His anger grew and he glanced at Rose, the lawyer, and to his surprise saw how his startlingly bright blue eyes were riveted on the speaker, his lips moving in unison with hers as he wordlessly echoed the ejaculations:

A Briton knows, or if he knows it not,
The Scripture plac'd within his reach, he ought,
That souls have no discriminating hue,
Alike important in their Maker's view;
That none are free from blemish since the fall,
And love divine has paid one price for all.

To Parker's even greater indignation, Rose then spoke.

'Miss Jane, forgive me, but you are so moved that I sense you are a trifle breathless. May I relieve you by completing the extract, though my recitation will be a pale shadow of your eloquence?'

Without waiting for a reply, without indeed requesting the volume of Cowper, he spoke from memory in the impassioned voice that he habitually reserved for closing arguments when pleading before the high courts of justice.

> The wretch that works and weeps without relief,
> *Has one that notices his silent grief,*
> *He from whose hands alone all pow'r proceeds,*
> *Ranks its abuse among the foulest deeds,*
> *Considers all injustice with a frown,*
> *But marks the man that treads his fellow down.*

Captain Parker could bear it no longer. He rose, bowed, mumbled his excuses and left the parlour. The party looked on in astonishment, with the exception of Mr. Rose and Jane, who looked at one another.

'It was very unfortunate that poor Captain Parker should be indisposed of a sudden. Perhaps he caught a chill or had eaten something disagreeable.' Her mother, often thinking herself an invalid, despite rude health, tended to side with the nervous or bilious.

'Perhaps William Cowper is not to his taste,' Jane replied.

The gentlemen had departed for billiards at the Shed and the ladies were taking their tea. The rain had finally stopped and a weak sun was dispersing the silvery-grey clouds. Now that Martha had rested following her journey, she was ready for a refreshing long walk in the late afternoon. Cassie offered to stay with her mother, so Jane and Martha set off, their thin wool cloaks billowing in the wind behind them.

They were finally alone. Martha was the first to speak. Of Captain Parker she had heard much, chiefly by letter. It was evident that he did admire her friend, but she was not so sure of Jane's feelings.

'What an agreeable man is Captain Parker,' Martha began cautiously. 'He is very much esteemed by your brother.'

'He seems a pleasant young man,' Jane agreed. 'Though we might differ in our taste for poetry.'

'That he admires you greatly is indubitable,' said Martha. 'No one who has seen you together could question his affection. He is good-looking, and rich, and universal reports of his courage exceed his reputation. Frank's account of his daring during the Battle of the Nile, and the esteem in which Lord Nelson holds him, are testament to him as a man of intrepidity and valour.'

'Of his heroism, I have no doubt,' Jane concurred. 'Nor of his taste for fashion. I have heard much of his gilt buttons, his gold lace edgings and white wool waistcoat lined with silk serge.'

By now they had approached the curve of the bay. The pink cliffs glowed in the evening light, casting its effervescence on the pale blue-grey water below.

'Does it not vastly invigorate the spirits, and the complexion, to breathe in the salt air and behold the beauties of the sea? I confess, I feel its effects at once,' cried Miss Lloyd, raising her voice to be heard against the crashing of the waves. The sun was beginning to set, illuminating the sky with shards of rose-gold embers, rippling onto the ocean. Arm in arm, they gazed out to the horizon, now in perfect, companionable silence, unbroken by nothing but the sound of the swell. It was Miss Lloyd who finally interrupted the quietude and turned to face her friend.

'You are too prudent to fall in love by the sea, Jane.'

She looked very well in pale-blue satin. Her long dark hair was coiled and set with a diamond bandeau that had once belonged to her aunt, Mrs. Cooper. The midweek ball had been a success, but she was out of spirits and depressed. She and Captain Parker had danced for much of the evening. The good reverend had discerned from the warmth and discretion of their greeting that Jane and Frank had respected his confidence regarding Leah. To

Jane's gratification, Frank had secured Martha for the first two dances. What a fine pair they made, and how happy her brother was putting his dancing skills to such good use. He was light on his feet, and as graceful as a stag. She felt all happiness for Martha, but for herself could feel none.

They had stayed late, until the moon appeared high over the still sea, throwing its silvery beam through the long windows of the Assembly Room. But she felt listless and dispirited, wandering from room to room in search of what she knew not.

The next morning, she rose early to mix her mother's laudanum drops, then retired to her chamber to read her novel, wishing only for silence and solitude.

No newspaper was delivered that morning. Martha and Cassie slept late. By the end of the morning Jane had completed the first volume of *Belinda*. It was her duty, she believed, to return the book, so that Mr. Rose could take his rightful turn. She must delay no more. Slipping out of the lodgings, she went to the circulating library. There was no one about, and all was deadly quiet. No, Mrs. Honeychurch had not had enquiries about Miss Edgeworth's novel. Yes, she could have volume two, with the greatest of pleasure. Though she lingered, she saw not a soul.

In the afternoon, she had planned on scribbling, but the words would not come. The heat was stifling, and she felt languid and full of ennui. Captain Parker had paid a morning visit while she was out, and she was thankful to have escaped. Last night at the ball, he had expressed his hope that he could see her alone. He was expecting a summons from Spithead any day. But he could not be avoided forever. She was grateful to be given an opportunity to speak alone with Miss Lloyd.

'Make haste, Martha. Come to the parlour.' Jane lost no time in relaying to her friend her suspicions that Parker was soon to make a proposal of marriage. Miss Lloyd had watched him carefully on his recent visits to Dove Lane and there was little doubt of his partiality for her friend. And yet there were moments when he looked at her with an expression that was dubitable. Parker's situation in life was most eligible, however, and Martha was determined to guide her friend with all that was rational and prudent. Jane's conduct with the Irish lawyer, Tom Lefroy, had not been beyond reproach, and though Martha believed it to have been no more than a flirtation, she had yet to discover whether lasting mischief had been done.

'Ah, it was my pride *only* that had been offended,' said Jane. 'Nor should I have wished to be settled in Ireland, so far from family and friends. There were no disappointed hopes, and I shall not censure him for caprice or instability. No, vanity, not love, was my folly.'

Martha was gratified to know that her friend's heart had remained unharmed and pressed her with equal firmness on whether she could love the captain.

'I am not insensible to the compliment of earning such a man's affection, but there is a complacency in his air and manner that does not denote fervent affection. There is a *something* lacking.'

'And you do not wish to disappoint the hopes of a most beloved brother?'

'Nor the expectations of parents who have sacrificed their home at least in part to promote their daughters' prospects and cease to be a burden on those who can ill-afford it.'

'How should you like the life of a sailor's wife? It is fraught with dangers, is it not? Would not you be excessively sorry to leave your dearest sister?'

'Naturally. But as soon as I find my sea legs, I should be comfortable in my wooden world. A well-stocked library will provide succour, and I should be sure to look the other way when a flogging is administered. Perhaps in Naples I shall meet his admired Lady Hamilton, and little Horatia, whom I'm told is very much like her father.'

Martha laughed. 'You're incorrigible, my dear. You must take this business of marriage and mothering seriously. Most of us only get one chance to succeed in love. If you *can* love Captain Parker, and he is of good countenance, well-informed and has captivating manners, then you must accept him. But I confess that I too am struck by something elusive in his address. There is a wariness in his eyes, do you not agree? Nevertheless, he prefers no other woman to you, of that I am sure.'

Despite her friend's misgivings, Jane *had* given the idea of a union with Captain Parker a great deal of rational thought. She knew she would be expected to sacrifice much, including her scribbling, which she felt sure he would not tolerate. And though he was a man of principle, there was the matter of the abolition, though she believed – or at least hoped – that she and Frank were making good ground in weakening his resolve. *That* was, she trusted, merely a matter of time. No, indeed, it was the very idea of giving oneself over completely to the beloved object, body and soul, that pricked at her consciousness. She was fond of her liberty, happy at home, and had not the least inclination to relinquish the advantages she enjoyed. Of domestic felicity, she had seen few examples that had compelled her to forgo her single state. Her thoughts had drifted to other unfortunate unions, such as that of her brother James and Mary. She reflected on how a weak match could bring out the very worst in a person, and how matches of interest, vanity or convenience diminished, instead of increased, happiness.

Misery in marriage *was* the greatest of all evils. She feared to indulge her romantic hopes of ever being loved by a man of superior genius and virtue with a temper and manner suited to her taste. In her heart, she knew her objections to Captain Parker could not be obviated, and therefore it was useless to state them; even to herself. And yet, thoughts of escape, of no longer being a burden on her beloved family, could not be eradicated.

Mr. William Swete was deep in conversation with his father. Frank, taking his morning walk on the sands to observe the sailboats, was made conscious of the raised voice of the former.

'I will not permit my own blood and substance to grovel in low insensibility or shame.'

'My dear boy, I approve very much of your sentiments respecting your child. It is surely incumbent on us to provide for our offspring whether black or white. She will be treated with the same kindness and attention as if she had been born in wedlock. In time she will be received at Oxton.'

'By keeping her at a distance from her own relations I think there is the greater chance of concealing from her her *inferiority* (to ape my mother's infelicitous phrasing) and preventing the mortification of being slighted by relations who from early habits she might consider herself perfectly on a footing with.'

Without wishing to cause embarrassment, Frank coughed as he approached the gentlemen and made his bow. He bade them a good morning and they exchanged a few pleasantries before William hurried away. The reverend spoke first.

'Captain Austen, I have to hope that my son's good nature will excuse the follies of youth, and to consider the provision here made as the most eligible atonement. We are all brethren – and children of one common parent. My wish is for my granddaughter to be trained up to the love and practice of virtue, and to be given a decent education in order to render her useful to society.'

Frank murmured his agreement. 'The bonds of family are powerful, Reverend Swete.'

'My son informs me that she excels at drawing. In this, she resembles her grandpapa. She does not yet speak. The long voyage aboard the *Eliza* was disagreeable. Storms raged in the northern seas, making the final leg treacherous. She has suffered much, I fear. Now he insists that she should not receive the smallpox inoculation.'

'The sea air will recover her health and spirits,' said Frank. 'She will breathe more freely in the pure air of this country.'

The reverend regarded him closely. He was an object of admiration, this calm and resolute young man.

'Let us contemplate the beauties of nature,' said Swete, with a sigh. 'What a bold and noble shore we see before us.'

They stood close enough to the foamy water's edge to feel the flecks of sea spray as they caught the rhythmic rumble of the waves, the swish, the silence, the roar. The sun on the sea glittered. Frank could taste the salt on his lips. Below him a lone sand crab scuttled away.

At once a thought occurred to him, a most capital thought. If he could be the conduit to facilitate this proposal, it might conceivably work. It would require the assistance of his sister, of course. But there was nobody better qualified to write such a letter. He must do it at once, without delay.

Captain Parker raised his glass to nobody in particular: 'Preserve us from the dangers of the sea and the violence of the enemy.' He took a long drink and slammed his glass on the table. The London was half empty, just as he liked it. By now he was much intoxicated. He had dined well on pigeon, peas, cold lamb and a tart. His thoughts turned to the events of the week. Rose was an impudent fool, appearing at the Austens unannounced with his newspaper and his vivid blue eyes that seemed to take in everything. They reminded Parker of another pair of fine eyes that had once transfixed him. But no more of that.

He had been taken by surprise with a paragraph in the morning's newspaper. It had chilled his bones. He must exercise the strictest caution. 'The teetotum keeps upright only when it spins,' he muttered. He took out a miniature that he kept with him, a small oval, inlaid with pearls. He rubbed his thumb gently over the glass where the eyes of the figure gazed out. Perhaps hazel eyes were the finest of all. He pressed the cold glass to his lips.

It was still light when he stumbled onto the sands, in search of fresh air to revive him. No cause to act like a tar captain, he admonished himself. He was an officer and a gentleman of the ocean. One of Lord Nelson's crocodiles. He glimpsed Reverend Swete and groaned. Now was not the time for the good reverend's prattle. The man was everywhere. Inescapable. Parker looked around, but there was nowhere to go, only the sands and sea stretched ahead. Swete, he could see, was not alone. He was in the company of a little girl with dark skin and curly hair. She was wearing a red wool spencer to keep out the cool night air. What a pretty child, he thought. And what was she doing here in Devon? Was she a servant child? He had little choice but to be introduced and make her acquaintance, and was astonished to discover that she was no more a servant than he was. She was, in truth, a near relation of the family. The reverend's pride in his son's daughter was much in evidence. The captain knelt on the sand and shook Leah's hand, his face a mask of inscrutability; he had practised long enough. Then, making a hasty bow, he hurried away towards his lodgings. He did not see the look of pity and compassion in the countenance of the goodly gentleman.

The Saturday morning sky was cornflower blue. He turned and walked to the eastern end of town, towards Otterton, away from the bathing machines, where the mouth of the River Otter crossed with a single bar to the open sea. All was solitary and quiet. The play of light on water shimmered and sparkled on the rippling surface. Removing his clothes, the captain plunged into the cold sea. He was a good swimmer and the water, milky-green, was soothing. He flipped onto his back, drinking in the ruby-red cliffs and the woods above.

'I have kept to my resolution,' said he aloud, though there was no one to hear him or hold him to account. The paragraph in the newspaper had rattled him, without a doubt. The men in question were known to him, and his heart flooded with pity and misery. His bare feet touched the sandy bottom and he shook his golden head, sending glistening droplets of water into the air. Tiny silvery fish swarmed in the clear shallows, tickling his legs. From the top of Peak Hill a gentleman watched. The captain had little idea that he was being observed. Nor would he have cared. In the ocean, he was free and safe from harm. The touch of the sea was sensuous, enfolding his body in its soft, close embrace.

Samuel Rose had also seen the paragraph that had so vexed his rival. For that reason he had refrained from sending the newspaper to Mr. Austen, not thinking it a suitable topic for the young ladies. Rose had been privy to reports regarding Captain Parker but was too judicious a man to pay attention to idle rumours. Ocular proof was more to his taste and judgement. Parker was discreet, to be sure. Rose's brow furrowed as he watched him swimming alone, his muscular arms beating against the waves. Well, he would leave him to his solitude. As Rose turned to walk away, he noticed another young gentleman, heading for the shore to bathe. He and Captain Parker were acquainted, so it would seem from the nod of familiarity given by the gentleman undressing on the shore. Samuel Rose narrowed his eyes in disbelief and apprehension as the scene unfolded, before turning away in pity and discomfort.

Jane would have been astonished to overhear her mother and father's conversation regarding the marriage prospects of their daughters. For all that Mrs. Austen professed herself no catch-match maker, she had experienced great pleasure when the engagement was announced between Cassie and Tom, no little sorrow at the thought of her daughter removing to Shropshire, and boundless compassion when the news of Tom's sudden death had reached Steventon. Mr. George Austen was fortunate in enjoying the excellent company of his girls and had no wish to see them settled away from him. The disadvantages of remaining single paled in comparison to those of an unhappy marriage. Yet he would always defer to his wife in such matters of the heart, for she was as good as she was sensible. She was rational enough to know that as girls of small fortune, their chances were circumscribed, but of health, sense and beauty she believed them to be rich. Cassie, it was true, was the beneficiary of a small annuity left to her by Tom, but she showed little inclination to marry.

Mrs. Austen was, nevertheless, excessively pleased with the admiration bestowed on her younger daughter by the agreeable Captain Parker. She had forgiven the incident at the card table, and he had had the good sense not to repeat his behaviour. Nor by now had it escaped her notice that Jane had also captured the attention of the lawyer, Mr. Rose. 'I think a little of the world would be a good thing for Jane to see before she makes her choice. It corrects romantic ideas, so natural and pleasant in youth,' said Mrs. Austen to her husband.

'I fear, should he choose her, she will not have him, though amiable and excellent,' replied Mr. Austen, who was much less secure of his daughter's romantic notions. 'She will not marry for worldly convenience, my dear. I will not deny that a woman or man who marries happily is much happier than anybody else. But the reverse! And the irrevocable nature of the connection is most alarming.'

His wife agreed. 'When it comes to marriage, a man undoubtedly risks a great deal, but allow me to say a woman risks still more.'

It was her husband's turn to agree. 'We must content ourselves that her money – or lack of – is not his object in paying her flattering attentions. He has asked me to let him come to speak to her this morning. I cannot mistake his meaning, which is, perhaps, a hasty one.'

'He is accustomed to making rapid decisions, my dear, on which the safety of his ship and crew depend. Sailors cannot afford to make long courtships in times of war.'

Her mind turned to the prospect of Martha and Frank. Martha was not pretty, but was so ladylike and agreeable.

'I cannot help hoping,' said Mrs. Austen, 'she is likely to do well and marry as happily as many girls who may have more personal beauty than she has. But, alas, she is poor and can scarcely afford a bone of mutton and potatoes as her dowry. The knife cuts the other way. Frank is in no position to take a wife. Captain Parker is fortunate in being a man of private fortune. He may make what choice he wishes.'

'Well, his spell ashore is coming to an end. Frank informs me that he has been recalled to the *Thrush*. The admiral is not a man any naval officer would wish to disappoint. But Jenny must decide for herself. Parker has a calm, decided temper and is not one open to dangerous impressions. He is a gentleman I trust with her happiness, if she can be persuaded. And as a particular friend of her brother, there is no impropriety in a hasty marriage.'

Mrs. Austen agreed.

'I think him uncommonly pleasing. There is such manliness and good sense, and freedom from all the vanities and littleness of his kind.' In private, she reflected to herself: I never saw anyone make so little effort to surmount any little cloud of *ennui* for the society he is in. Of the cause of his enervation, she could not guess. She could hope only that marriage to her lively daughter would be the means of restoring his happiness.

Mr. Rose carried a goldfish in a pail. It was a sultry Sunday morning, but he was wrapped in a light wool comforter. His troublesome cough had worsened, despite the sea air and the ministrations of his physician, yet the fatigue he had laboured under when he arrived in Devonshire had dissipated. He felt renewed, invigorated and full of purpose.

That morning he had written again to Mr. Hayley, recounting the secret that the Reverend Swete had imparted to him at the midweek ball, his tongue loosened by several bowls of punch: the true identity of the girl on the beach. The child's very existence was the strongest proof of all that they had fought for and canvassed. Their beloved poet had not lived to see the fruits of his labours, but Hayley's *Life and Posthumous Writings of William Cowper Esq.* would make amends and seal William's name among the great abolitionists, helped in small part by the addition of Mr. Rose's own reminiscences and cache of letters from dear Cowper. All in good time, he said to himself.

As he strolled across the Mall, the lawyer reflected upon the Swete family and the manner in which they had responded to Leah. The son needed purpose and there was no doubting that fatherhood had been the means of improving him considerably. The girl's grandfather had begun to instruct her in the art of watercolour, for which she showed great aptitude. Leah was still silent as the grave, but Rose had heard peals of laughter when her grandpapa swept her up in his arms and placed her on his donkey's back. Amelia Swete was another matter. She showed no sign of relenting her stance of open hostility towards the blameless child.

When Rose arrived at his destination, he perceived that someone else had preceded him. To his astonishment, Miss Jane Austen was kneeling on the sands and speaking to Leah with her fingers. She looked up at the gentleman as he approached. 'It's how I speak with my poor brother, George. You will not be aware that he has an incapacity and no longer lives with the family. I find the hands a most efficacious medium of communication, Mr. Rose. To employ them feelingly dispenses with so much cold formality, do you not think?'

'I do not doubt it,' he replied, barely able to contain his surprise. He felt uncommonly foolish standing there holding his bucket, the water sloshing over its sides onto the sand.

'My brother is inspecting the herring nets, as is his wont,' she explained, with a wave of her hand towards the fishermen's cottages, 'leaving me free to converse with Miss Swete in blissful silence.'

'You are fond of children, Miss Jane?'

'Naturally. I take my position of *Aunt* with great seriousness. Now do you bring your pail to make castles of sand? You must take care not to build your foundations too close to the water's edge for fear they will be swept away into the ocean!'

She's laughing at me, thought Rose. He had never met a woman like her in his life.

Leah had risen to her feet to peer into the bucket. She exclaimed with delight when she saw the bright fish darting around its circumference. Rose handed her the present with a graceful bow and a nod to her governess, who hurried over to examine the contents, thanking him again and again for his kindness.

'Would you permit me to accompany you?' said he to Jane, who nodded her head in agreement, as they walked westwards, her pink parasol flapping in the salty breeze. She had no intention of speaking another syllable. If the silence was uncomfortable, then so be it. Once again, he had shown an irritating ability to turn up unexpectedly and disturb her peace.

'How does Captain Parker do?' he broke out, fiddling with his watch and chain, longing to warn her of the dangers that lay ahead. She was too fine a young woman to be preyed upon in such a manner that could result only in abject misery and humiliation, yet he felt himself too inextricably bound to be objective.

She looked at him with surprise.

'I beg your pardon,' said he, a crimson stain flushing his countenance. 'It is no business of mine.'

'To my knowledge, sir, Captain Parker does very well. As the particular friend of my *brother*, and a gentleman of easy and pleasing manners, he is a most welcome addition to our circle at home. He will be sorely missed when he is recalled to the *Thrush*.'

'I doubt not that,' said Rose miserably. He knew all

was lost and that she would unite herself to an unworthy, dishonest and troubled man who would forever disturb her peace.

'Do not marry him.'

'I beg *your* pardon, Mr. Rose?'

'Do not marry him.'

'It can be of no consequence to you, or to anyone, whom I chose to marry. Your impertinence astounds me. What can this mean?'

'You know not what you do. I implore you not to ask me to explain,' said he, fixing his eyes on hers, assailed at once by the confusion and astonishment in her expression. With a sigh, he turned, made an elegant bow and walked away, leaving his footprints in the wet sand.

Before relating the details of this strange encounter to Martha and Cassie, Jane removed her bonnet and hung it on the stand in the hallway. Mr. and Mrs. Austen were taking their daily walk to the Shed, so the young women had Dove Lane to themselves.

Martha had been baking and the warm yeasty smell of bread hung about the room. A large seed cake was cooling on the kitchen table. She was copying a receipt – one of Frank's favourites – into her household book, saying aloud as she wrote, 'Cut two chickens as for fricasseeing, wash them clean and put them in a stew pan with as much water as will cover them ... half a pound of fresh butter in the pan and brown it a little ... two cloves of garlic ... two or three spoonfuls of curry powder ... let all stew till tender. If acid is agreeable squeeze the juice of a lemon or orange into it ...'

Jane waited for her to put down her pen. Then she spoke. Martha and Cassie listened with incredulity and concern.

'Poor Mr. Rose,' Cassie began. 'He is a gentleman whose veracity cannot be questioned, and though he has overcome the bounds of decorum there must be some mistake, some misapprehension.'

'Perhaps Captain Parker is secretly engaged?' Martha suggested. 'If so, he has done you wrong. It is distressing. One does not know what to think.'

Jane took off her pale-green slippers, tapping out the silvery sand grains onto a sheet of newspaper. Cassie removed her sister's damp white stockings.

'You are mistaken, my dear Martha,' said Jane. 'One knows exactly what to think. Mr. Rose has no business giving unsolicited advice to a woman with whom he is barely acquainted and whose opinion has not been sought. It is behaviour of the most provoking kind and is not to be tolerated.'

Cassie and Martha exchanged a glance.

'I had absolutely decided on refusing Captain Parker but now I am not so sure. Perhaps, after all, I am suited to be the wife of a sailor. Perhaps I shall marry him to spite Mr. Rose. Happiness in marriage is entirely a matter of chance, and the less one knows about the other the better.'

'You cannot believe that, dear Jane,' said Cassie. 'That is not your creed.' She did not say what she felt, that she had known what it was to love a man with every pore of her being and to feel that she would never look upon his like again; that she would rather be poor and a spinster than marry a man she could not love or esteem.

Jane regarded closely the two women in the chamber. Cassie bravely carrying her loss with such fortitude. Martha loving Frank from afar, like Patience on a Monument, while he barely gave her a second look. Her eyes filled unexpectedly with tears at the hopelessness of it all.

'How preferable it would be,' said she, 'to have a solid roof over one's head, a desk to write at, and the happiness to be at leisure to live in peace and solitude. To be rich is a blessing.'

'Let us read one of your volumes, Jane,' said Martha. 'Captain Parker will soon arrive and a calm disposition will enable you to make a rational decision.' Cassie agreed that reading was the best remedy for agitated emotions and went to fetch one of her sister's manuscripts from her writing box. Jane felt grateful for the soothing presence of Cassie and Martha. They understood her more completely than anyone else, even her beloved Frank.

How right they were! There was no gentleman *alive* who could obstruct her enjoyment of reading. No one who could make unpleasant ideas dissipate in the manner of an enjoyable book. She was still at leisure to think and read. Martha began chapter one of *First Impressions* in her lilting, clear voice. Jane rose and walked to the window.

'It's beginning to rain,' said she.

Mr. Rose decided on a final course of action. How to convey such melancholy intelligence in a manner befitting a gentleman, he knew not. But of its necessity he was utterly convinced. He begged Captain Austen's pardon but he came on a matter of the utmost importance, and concerned the happiness of a most beloved sister. Frank ushered him into his cottage from the heavy rain and bade him sit by the fire.

The lawyer accepted the wine that Frank offered with grateful thanks, struck anew by the resemblance between brother and sister; the bright intelligence of the hazel eyes, the dark chestnut hair.

When Mr. Rose had finished his narrative, Frank looked at the paragraph the assiduous lawyer had so carefully cut from the *Hampshire Chronicle*. His heart ached for his friend.

Monday morning John Hubbard and George Hynes, two seamen belonging to the St George, were executed on board that ship, in this harbour, pursuant to their sentence, for an unnatural crime.

He had remained silent while Rose relayed what he had seen at the beach. Frank tore the fragment into tiny pieces and threw them into the fire.

Rose was manifestly a principled man, no idle tattler. He had spoken with a degree of sensibility and rationality that could brook no dissent. He had answered Frank's careful and precise questions with candour and fidelity. There was no mischief here. Nothing had been exaggerated, inflated or distorted. It was the plain, unvarnished truth. Frank felt that he had blinded himself to his friend's character and had encouraged a union that could bring only misery and humiliation to both parties.

The prospect could not be more grave. Yet it was too late. At that very moment, Parker was pressing his suit and he had every reason to believe he would be accepted. His sister's fate was decided. Frank turned to the lawyer.

'One final question, Mr. Rose. I am a plain-speaking man and there is something that puzzles me exceedingly.

Why especially should you concern yourself with the happiness and peace of my sister?'

'I bathed and had a glorious tumble in the waves,' said Captain Parker as he was ushered into the parlour where Jane was waiting.

He had not the least doubt of being accepted if he made a proposal of marriage and was certain of being favourably received by the entire family. This was his best hope of safety. His best hope of survival. If he felt a prick of conscience at using his friend's sister so abominably, it was pushed to one side. He had loved Frank so well and so long, he could love the sister. Marriage would be the making of him. He could begin anew and leave behind the old life. She would give him the chance of repenting and making amends before it was too late.

He thought she was looking particularly lovely in her pink dress, trimmed with white ribbon. She received him warmly, taking his coat and hat, soaked through with rain. He sat down on the sofa beside the blazing fire. They both knew what was expected.

'Are you in earnest, Miss Austen?'

'Perfectly in earnest, Captain Parker.'

'That shows your good sense, as well as your good nature. Never was any human being less bent on falling in love than I when I arrived at Sidmouth.'

'I am not, I think, very romantic, for I do not think *violent love* necessary to one's happiness, but I think you will agree with me that a *decided preference* is absolutely so.'

He nodded his agreement. She continued.

'I believe that half the miseries of the world arise from foolish mysteries, from the want of courage to speak the truth.'

There was a long pause. The captain was unable to meet her eye. He shifted in his seat. Then he dropped to his knees.

'Miss Austen, Jane. I am ashamed of my weakness.'

'You have no cause, Captain Parker. It is the outward life that conforms and the inward life that questions.'

'My conduct and feelings being so natural to me, insomuch as they were not taught, but instinctive ...'

'I understand. I wish you every happiness, Captain. And I have a duty to protect my own. Nothing can be compared to the misery of being bound *without* love, bound to one and preferring another. That is a punishment that neither of us deserves.'

He could say nothing, his heart was so full. He was filled with gratitude and wonder at her equanimity. How she had penetrated his secret, seemingly by instinct alone, he could not know. He kissed her hand. For her part, she did not repine. She could feel only compassion for him, for Frank and for herself. It was a providential escape from wretchedness for life.

WEEK FOUR

The state of slavery is of such a nature, that it is incapable of being introduced on any reasons, moral or political ... It is so odious, that nothing can be suffered to support it.

(Lord Mansfield)

Dear Lady Brocas,

I hope this letter finds you in the most excellent spirits, and in the enjoyment of the beauty of Wokefield Park.

I trust you will excuse the liberty I take in addressing you on a matter of considerable personal and delicate interest, and which I am persuaded only your unparalleled compassion and kindness could so generously embrace.

I write to you from this charming seaside resort, at Sidmouth, where the salt air and gentle breezes have done wonders for my health. It is in this tranquil setting that I have found myself drawn into the affairs of a most amiable gentleman, Reverend Swete, whose kindness and good nature have endeared him to all who know him.

Mr. Swete has confided in me a matter that weighs heavily upon his heart. His son, a young man of wayward disposition, has found himself entangled in the complexities of life in Antigua. The consequence of his indiscretions is a daughter, a sweet girl of tender years, and the child of a slave who has now died. I cannot but feel the deepest sympathy for this young creature, deprived of the tender care and guidance that every child deserves.

The gentleman has made every effort to provide for the child, but he is keenly aware that her prospects and social standing would benefit immensely from the nurturing care of someone of refined and respectable circumstances. It is here that your benevolence and personal experience would make such a profound difference.

I am most respectfully requesting that you might consider taking this young girl under your protection and guidance. In offering this request, I am motivated by a sincere wish for the child's future happiness and success, knowing how much she would benefit from the life and opportunities afforded by Wokefield Park. I am assured that the young girl would be welcomed with open arms and heartened by the knowledge of your own distinguished heritage and kind-hearted nature.

Should you deem this proposal agreeable, I am happy to provide any further information and to facilitate the arrangements necessary for her transfer. Your favourable consideration of this matter would greatly ease the anxieties of her loving grandfather and secure the child's future with the comfort and stability she so deserves.

I know that this is a great deal to ask, and I beg your forgiveness for imposing upon your kindness. Yet, I cannot shake the feeling that this is a matter of the utmost importance, and that you are the only person who can truly make a difference in this young girl's life.

I remain, with the highest regard and most earnest hope for your favourable reply,

Yours most sincerely,

Jane Austen

Wokefield Park was situated in the county of Berkshire. Handsomely built in the Palladian style and set in two hundred and fifty acres of parkland, landscaped with avenues, woodland and water, the mansion was in the possession of the Brocas family, who had added three-storey wings to the left and right of the main building. However, by far its most prominent feature was a gateway designed for Lady Sarah Brocas – a pair of elaborate wrought-iron gates, supported by tall, brick pillars, each emblazoned with a new family crest: the proud, noble visage of an African male wearing an eastern coronet, a tribute to the new bride of Bernard Brocas.

She was an exceedingly wealthy West Indian Creole, Sarah Redhead, the natural daughter of Samuel Redhead, plantation owner. More than a few elegant eyebrows had been raised when Bernard Brocas, himself a natural son, had inherited Wokefield. But when he brought back his raven-haired bride, tongues had wagged in the salons of polite society.

Her inheritance of half a million pounds superseded comments about her obscure origins. Sir Bernard took no heed, and set about improving the interior of Wokefield, installing extensive wooden panelling and a marble fireplace. His final commission was a full-length portrait of Lady Brocas, fashionably dressed in pink figured sarsenet and bedecked with brilliants. A cluster of creamy pearls encircled her throat, offsetting her light-brown complexion.

Just this morning Lady Brocas had received a letter from Miss Jane Austen, the neighbour of her husband's mother, Lady Harriet, at whose estate, Beaurepaire in Hampshire, James Austen was curate. Though the families were thus connected, they were not intimate acquaintances, so the lady of Wokefield was surprised, and intrigued, by the contents of the letter.

Lady Brocas folded the letter and placed it in her bureau. Having been brought to England herself, educated and introduced into society, she felt a profound obligation to render similar service to the child. She would make the necessary enquiries before uprooting the girl and removing her from her own relations, but in her heart her decision was made. Nonetheless, she was loath to gain the reputation of providing succour for every orphaned heiress from the West Indies, or she would have a house full!

Lady Brocas could not decide whether Jane Austen's letter was proof of her impertinence, or her good heart.

Their fourth week by the sea began with a few days of summer skies. Kingfisher blue in the morning turned to cobalt in the afternoon heat. The ruddy cliffs were fringed and overhung with a large mass of brushwood, ivy and grass, which was being daily diminished by the buffeting of the waves. At the ebb of the tide, a fine strand, well suited for exercise or amusement, stretched onwards, halfway to Budley Point.

'What dreadful hot weather we have! It keeps one in a continual state of inelegance,' said Jane to Cassie. She wondered if she dared to slip off her stockings and shoes, to feel the cool sand beneath her feet.

Later in the week they awoke to rain. In the afternoon it cleared; the wind changed into a softer quarter, the clouds were carried off; the sun appeared; it was summer again. Jane resolved to be out of doors as soon as possible. Never had the sight, smell, sensation of nature, tranquil, warm and brilliant after a storm, been more attractive to her. She had confessed everything only to her sister, who felt pity for Captain Parker. She was comforted to hear that he was no object of regret.

'I am not in want of that sort of compassion,' said Jane. 'My vanity was flattered, and I allowed his attentions. Latterly, however – for some time, indeed – I have had no idea of their meaning any thing – I thought them a habit, a trick, nothing that called for seriousness on my side. He has imposed on me, but he has not injured me. I have never been attached to him. He never wished to attach me. It was merely a blind to conceal his real situation with another.'

Frank, when he heard of his sister's refusal, was simply relieved to discover that her heart had not been harmed. 'Peter has been playing a most dangerous game,' said he. 'No judge of his manners to you. Always deceived in fact by his own wishes, and regardless of little besides his own convenience. Fancying you to have fathomed his secret.'

'There are secrets in all families, my dear Frank.'

'My only comfort is that I am fortunate that your affections were not further entangled! – I could never, I confess, from your manners, assure myself as to the degree of what you felt – I could only be certain that there was a preference.' Jane assured him that this was not the case and that Captain Parker had suffered, and would continue to suffer.

Frank had not disclosed the role that Mr. Rose had played in the unravelling of Parker's perfidy. Knowing Jane's dislike of the lawyer, he felt that little could be gained from the intelligence. She had seen nothing of Rose, despite her frequent trips to the circulating library, having now obtained the third and final volume of *Belinda*. She had asked herself if he was avoiding her company; it required effort in such a small town, to evade her presence. Jane wondered if he would attend the midsummer night ball.

Now that Martha, and the rest of the family, knew of Jane's rejection of Captain Parker, she was grateful that they asked no questions and that her 'No' was enough. Mrs. Austen had given a quizzical look to her husband, who simply responded that Jenny must do what she thought best. Martha's discreet nature rendered her determined to seek no particulars. The siblings were relieved. They had no wish to see the captain suffer the fate of the two sailors in Hampshire.

The midsummer assembly was a welcome relief to all. Jane dressed carefully in her sprigged muslin with blue trimmings. Scouring the crowded ballroom, her eyes alighted upon the object of her thoughts, not three yards from where she stood. He moved closer to her and, with an air of solicitude, began in a tone of anxiety to enquire after her health. Jane replied in the affirmative, and he asked if she would stand up with him. She accepted, grateful for his silence and for the lightness of his touch upon her hand. His presence was soothing, consoling. A few minutes passed pleasantly, before he spoke.

'Do you find Sidmouth as agreeable as when I had the honour of making the enquiry before?'

'Yes, quite, Mr. Rose – more so, indeed.'

'How does your brother do? Does he continue in town?'

'He does, though any minute he expects a call to Plymouth.'

'Have you gone on with Miss *Belinda*? I must extend my thanks to you for returning volume one in such excellent condition. Not a single tearstain in evidence.'

'She is a great pleasure to me. Though I confess the heroine is a little *too good* for my liking. Lady Delacour is, perhaps, more to my taste.'

'Ah, Lady Delacour, a noted wit and incorrigible coquette, whose main object in life is to excite her husband's jealousy and prove her dominance over her lord and master.'

'Surely you do not think that a wife is a being whose actions are necessarily governed by a husband, Mr. Rose. Or that a witty woman is to be regarded as an object of ridicule?'

'Not at all. Pray, do not misunderstand me. Perhaps no kind of superiority is more flattering or alluring than that which is conferred by the powers of conversation, by extemporaneous sprightliness of fancy, copiousness of language and fertility of sentiment.'

She smiled in agreement as they reached the bottom of the set.

'You dance very well, Mr. Rose, perhaps with as much elegance as you converse.'

'*You* have too much wit to be a good flatterer.'

'And, perhaps, you think too much to make a good friend?'

'Not so,' said he. 'I would at any time rather be cut by a sharp knife than by a blunt one.'

Here their conversation closed, the demands of the dance becoming too importunate for a divided attention.

Of a sudden, a hush descended upon the ballroom, followed by murmurings. Jane had broken off from Mr. Rose to stand next to Lady Grosvenor, who was expensively dressed and bedecked in brilliants and whose loud whispers penetrated the company.

Reverend Swete had entered with two of his grown-up daughters and a little girl dressed in white satin, with pink trimmings. He guided her gently towards the dancers. The child looked at them in fascination.

Her first ball, thought Jane, her heart rising. And perhaps her grandfather's wish that she attend.

'Look at the Reverend's black princess,' said Lady Grosvenor. 'I wonder who will be brave enough to stand up with her.'

Jane turned to her sister, 'Surely it must be the fashion to be very affected or very rude, there seems to be no medium between these extremes.'

In the next instant, she saw Mr. Rose making his way across the ballroom. Before she knew it, he was leading Leah to the top of the set. Jane was astonished. That he had asked Miss Swete to stand up with him, paying no heed to the insolent stares of the crowd, and singling her out for special attention was a source of surprise and delight. It was proof of his good nature.

'You cannot wonder at my thinking of the title in the song *Sure such a pair were never seen,*' said Lady Grosvenor with a sneer.

Jane was gratified to discover that Mr. Rose was to be her supper partner. His conversation was of a different sort to that of young men in general, and never had she passed two or three hours at a ball more pleasantly. He talked with fluency and spirit, and she was struck by his intelligent and lively eyes. She began to think him uncommonly pleasing. She had praised him for his kind attentions to Miss Swete, and he had accepted the compliment with an artlessness and humility that was most becoming.

'Others should take a lesson in the art of obliging,' she remarked, with a sigh.

He replied that there was, indeed, no sense of obligation, only of pleasure, and turned the conversation to herself and her situation in life.

'I have much to say, as people usually have when they begin to talk about themselves,' said she. She found herself confessing to him her scribbling habit and his generous curiosity stimulated her regard. The conversation turned to female novel writers.

'Is it necessary to discard the title of *novel* because many bad novels are in existence?' she cried.

'Ah, you mean Miss Edgeworth, do you not? It is not strange that she adopts the appellation – "a moral tale" – and yet, despite her protestations, her villainess is more attractive than her heroine. A prude is a character more suspected by men of the world than even a coquette.'

'Belinda *is* perhaps a little too cool, and reserved. But it is surely the growth of the heroine's mind that interests?'

'She transfers her affection from one man to another, and then back again, such is the charge of inconstancy that I bring against our fair heroine.'

'The unpleasantness of appearing fickle is certainly great,' Jane agreed. 'Whether romantic love is to be experienced only once, and precludes happiness and contentment in subsequent relationships, is perhaps a matter to be addressed. The authoress shows that a second and more rational affection might lead to a more successful conclusion. But remember, Mr. Rose, we have not yet completed the final volume.'

'One further question in the case for the prosecution, Miss Austen. In the words of the character, Miss Harriet Freke, why, O why, when a woman likes a man, does not she go and tell him so honestly?'

'Because if she be a woman of sense, she would know that by such a step she would disgust the object of her affection. Perhaps a woman should never show feelings she ought not to express.'

'You cannot mean that. Though I confess that the man who thinks of a wife is a very strict observer of her manners, however he may seem enamoured. But I cannot think so badly of my own sex. You have perhaps a prejudice in favour of your own?'

'We are all apt to think that an opinion that differs from our own is a prejudice,' said she with a smile. She rose from the table, permitting him to draw her shawl across her shoulders.

'One final word, Miss Jane, before you join your sister. Allow me to close this most interesting conversation with a phrase of Miss Edgeworth's: *That love is most to be valued which cannot be easily won.*'

'The more I see of him, the more I like him; it's most vexing,' said she to Cassie.

'That was not your first impression, my dear. I wonder what it is that has changed your mind.'

'Were he an Adonis, my dear sister, he would not have made any impression on me instantly. We gradually acquire a knowledge of the good qualities of those who endeavour to please us, and if they are really amiable, their persons become agreeable to us by degrees.'

'You were roused by his kind attentions to Miss Swete, confess?'

'Those fine *ladies* begging for their smelling salts have no business at a public ball. Miss Swete is a delightful child and nothing could have pleased me more than Mr. Rose's complaisance.'

'And his being a friend of your most beloved poet, no doubt, adds to his many charms?'

'Mr. Rose has promised to show me some of his letters from William Cowper, and their mutual affection is indeed pleasing and raises him in my esteem.'

'How long does he stay at Sidmouth?'

'He is preparing to depart to Sussex, for the trial of Mr. Blake. But he assures me that he will return to Devon.'

'He will be a loss to our little society. And Frank and Martha to depart so soon. He to Plymouth and she to Hampshire. All ideas of romance between *them* at an end. And, my dear, I must beg you to take care and be prudent. Admiration can be just that, and not proof of an attachment.'

Jane assured her sister that she was in no danger, that her affections were guarded and that she had no reason to be displeased with her conduct. In fact, she felt sure she had behaved with a coolness that had convinced him they were to be no more than friends.

'All of these help,' said Cassie, 'but still the danger does not lie in any of them, but in a nameless, indescribable *something* that winds round and round one, as silk round a silkworm, and becomes entangled, irretrievably so, before one is aware where one is.'

Cassie, who *had* been in love, was not at all convinced by her sister's protestations. She had not seen a man equal to Mr. Rose in temper, feelings, education, principles and understanding, and his being a man of large fortune meant that he would not throw himself away on a seaside romance. His plan to leave for Sussex was a consolation and would give her sister time for reflection. The family were to return to Bath within the fortnight, yet she felt Jane's tranquillity and peace stood a better chance if they were to part at once.

Mr. George Austen had made the relevant enquiries and satisfied himself that Mr. Samuel Rose was a gentleman from a very respectable family in Chiswick in Middlesex. His father, Doctor William Rose, a native of Scotland, led an academy during many years, with considerable emolument and unblemished reputation. Mr. Samuel Rose was the heir at law to an uncle, from whom he had inherited a private fortune and a house in Devonshire. Samuel was an only son, raised with fond and successful care by a parent who had devoted the chief attention of a very active, benevolent and cheerful mind to the important duties of education. After completing his studies at the university in Edinburgh, he entered his name at Lincoln's Inn and devoted himself to the law, a line of life for which he seemed equally prepared by nature and nurture. Being called to the bar in 1796, he had attached himself to the home circuit and to the sessions of Sussex.

Swete, overcome with gratitude for Rose's intervention at the ball, had been only too glad to vouchsafe for the young lawyer.

'He is admired for the rare talent of examining a witness with a becoming mixture of acuteness and humanity. With such a mind, with a fund of classical learning and of general knowledge, with an early command of language, and with manners peculiarly conciliating, he has everything to hope,' said the reverend.

'My daughter informs me that he was a friend to poor Mr. Cowper, and now Mr. Hayley; writers that she greatly esteems.'

'Indeed, my dear sir. Samuel Rose is distinguished by that turn of mind of an eager, yet a modest desire to cultivate the acquaintance of men who had risen to eminence by their intellectual endowments.'

'A taste for literature adds much to the happiness of life,' agreed Mr. Austen.

The reverend had heard that despite a considerable portion of bodily strength and agility, Rose was at Sidmouth for the restitution of his health, for boxing exercises, in which he excelled, and for the benefits of fresh air and the waters. Apparently he had been afflicted since an early age with periodical headaches of extreme severity.

'His profession is arduous, but he would not hear of quitting it for a less active one without exposing himself to some degree of discredit,' said the reverend. 'He is a most amiable gentleman and a highly promising character, destined to rise by sure, though slow, degrees to the highest honours of his profession.'

Mr. Austen made his thanks for the intelligence. His Jenny could not be happy with a man unworthy of her talents, whatever great wealth and amiability he may have. George Austen had early recognised something distinctive in his daughter's abilities and had furnished her with those things necessary for her ambition: her notebooks, her desk, her writing box. His wife had granted her daughter the hours to write, sparing her from household duties. Mr. Cadell was a fool, of course, to refuse her manuscript. But Jenny had laughed it off and become only more determined to find another publisher. Bath would provide opportunities, George mused. Another good reason to be out of the countryside and into the city, where her gifts would flourish!

Quite how a husband would fit into the picture was not yet evident. Her refusal of Captain Parker suggested to him that his daughter's hand was not easily to be won.

'Jane,' Cassandra ventured, her blue eyes soft with sisterly amusement, 'you have adjusted that ribbon twice already. Shall I declare you unsettled?'

Jane's fingers stilled over the ribbon that adorned her light muslin gown. 'Unsettled? Dearest Cassandra, I do hope you are not so easily deceived by appearances,' she replied, feigning a serenity she did not quite possess.

Cassie laughed gently. 'Oh, but I am! For I know you too well. And perhaps I am equally deceived by the evident good opinion Mr. Rose holds of you, which may yet prove an enticement to the heart of my dear sister.'

Jane was saved the necessity of a retort, for at that very moment a rustle of boots and the creak of the door announced the arrival of Mr. Rose. He entered with a countenance flushed not from exertion, but from the agreeable eagerness of bearing good news. His eyes, always so keen and earnest in conversation, shone with pleasure. In one hand he carried his hat and in the other a small volume, his fingers drumming lightly upon its leather cover.

'Miss Austen, Miss Jane,' said he, bowing with deference to both sisters, 'I bring intelligence. A company of players has arrived in Sidmouth. They shall this very Saturday evening be performing Goldsmith's *She Stoops to Conquer* in the Assembly Rooms.'

Jane's eyes sparkled with interest. '*She Stoops to Conquer*,' she repeated. 'I had not expected such a diversion in this quiet retreat. Do you speak truly, Mr. Rose?'

'Most truly,' he assured her. 'And by good fortune I encountered your father on the Mall and he granted me permission to accompany you both to the performance. I understand, Miss Jane, that you are an enthusiast for the stage. Have I the happiness of hearing that you approve of Goldsmith's works?'

'Some of his works, but not all of them.'

Mr. Rose looked crestfallen, while Cassie exchanged a sly glance with Jane. 'You must forgive my sister, but she has a low opinion of Goldsmith's *History of England*.'

'It was a favourite of my father, but I was vexed and wearied by the quarrels of popes and kings, the wars and pestilence on every page; the men all so good for nothing, and hardly any women at all.'

'Hardly any women at all? That cannot be said of his plays.'

With this, Rose handed her the small volume.

Jane turned to the title page: '*The Miscellaneous Works of Oliver Goldsmith, Volume Two: Dramatic.* Why, that is very kind of you, Mr. Rose. Do you suspect that I am in need of a promptbook for tonight? I can assure you that *She Stoops to Conquer* was a firm favourite at Steventon.'

With a shy smile, he replied, 'I prepared this edition myself.'

Jane was all amazement.

'You are a busy man,' said Cassie.

'The law court by day and the scholar's study at night?' added Jane. 'I shall greatly enjoy these *miscellaneous* works.'

The evening's arrangements were made with mutual goodwill, and Samuel Rose departed, his step noticeably lighter. Cassie resumed her needlework and lifted her eyes to Jane. 'Well, sister, I surmise that, though you have not stooped, you have conquered.'

A makeshift stage had been erected at one end of the Assembly Rooms and benches filled the dance-floor. Gentlemen and ladies streamed through the grand entrance, their voices rising in happy exclamation, fans fluttering like butterflies in the warm air. Chandeliers glittered from above, casting a golden glow over the audience, arrayed in all the finery of seaside fashion. Amid the laughter and general air of expectation, Jane felt her spirits rise, turning to delight when word spread through the room that Tony Lumpkin was to be played by John Quick, who had created the role.

'I do prefer a laughing to a sentimental comedy,' said she to Mr. Rose, but before he could reply, the play began on a stage set to resemble a chamber in an old-fashioned house – the home of Mr. and Mrs. Hardcastle and their vivacious daughter Kate.

'I vow, Mr. Hardcastle, you're very particular. Is there a creature in the whole country but ourselves, that does not take a trip to town now and then, to rub off the rust a little? There's the two Miss Hoggs, and our neighbour Mr. Grigsby, go to take a month's polishing every winter.'

There was a cheer when Quick made his first appearance. Though he was now well past his prime, his roguish grin, expertly timed gestures and clownish turns of phrase conspired to keep the audience in fits of laughter. Every now and then, Jane glanced at Mr. Rose. She suspected that he saw something of himself in the play's bashful hero, Marlow, who was uncomfortable in the presence of fine ladies. As Marlow was more at ease in conversation with an innkeeper or a barmaid, was Rose his true self only with his impoverished clients, such as poor Mr. Blake?

At the interval, Samuel escorted the sisters into the crowd gathered near the refreshment tables. 'Mr. Lewis does not disappoint, does he?' said he.

'Gentleman Lewis has retained all his refinement, but is he not a little advanced in age to represent the young hero? He must have been playing the role for nigh on thirty years.' Rose laughed, as Jane continued, 'But age cannot wither nor custom stale the brilliance of John Quick.'

'And the mistaken identities,' said Samuel, with a lawyer's appreciation for trickery and disguises. 'What an ingenious device! How artfully Goldsmith handles the deception, weaving humour through every layer of the misunderstanding.'

Cassie looked intently at the pair of them. 'It is singular that the character of Marlow reveals that even a gentleman who struggles to express his feelings may become himself – in the right company.'

As the second half began, the humour and charm of Goldsmith's world drew them in once more. Jane, caught between the enchantment of the performance and the agreeable presence of Mr. Rose beside her, was in the happiest of tempers.

After the actors had taken their final bows, the audience flocked into the lantern-lit street, the cool breeze from the sea a pleasant contrast to the heat of the Assembly Rooms. Samuel offered his arm to both sisters and as they strolled towards their lodgings, conversation flowed as easily as the waves lapping the shore.

'The charm of Goldsmith's wit,' said Jane, her voice soft and thoughtful, 'is surely in the way he brings all his characters to a level footing, for better or worse. The follies of the gentry are revealed just as readily as those of the lower classes, and yet he does so with such kindness.'

Samuel Rose looked at her with admiration. 'Indeed, you have the very heart of the matter, Miss Jane. Goldsmith's humour is always tempered with humanity. He makes us laugh, yet he never wounds.'

'Perhaps that is the highest aim of any writer,' said she, as Rose escorted them to their door – 'to make one feel the laughter of life, without ever making one feel ashamed.'

'Even Jane cannot refuse a second suitor in one week,' said Mrs. Austen to her husband. 'She may never receive another proposal, and good ones are as rare as hen's teeth for young ladies with no dowries.'

'Perhaps Mr. Rose may succeed where his rival has failed. He is not a man to subdue her spirit. He is a man of good principles. And, I trust, religion.'

George Austen was sitting by the fire, the day's news and his spectacles in hand.

Cassandra caught the gist of their conversation as she entered the parlour. 'Today is the day that he departs for Sussex.'

'Well, I daresay he has business to attend to,' said Mr. Austen. 'A man cannot reside eternally by the sea merely for the sake of fresh air, however amiable the company.'

'My love, I am persuaded that the young man's attentions have been sufficiently marked as to suggest he cannot long bear to be separated from Jane. It is possible – nay, probable – that he intends a brief retreat to reflect upon the constancy of his own attachment.'

'I should like to think as much, Mama,' said Cassie, 'but have you not heard, on every side, of gentlemen who quit town, never to return? They leave – professing love, hinting at marriage – and their promises dissolve into mist and empty breezes.'

'I do not believe, my dear,' said her father, 'that Mr. Rose's character is quite so fickle.'

At that moment, the very gentleman of whom they spoke was announced. He had come to make his farewell before leaving for Sussex. Permission to walk along the sands with Miss Jane was readily given and the two set off. It was a day of glowering clouds and summer squalls. The waves crashed against the pebbles.

'Of all horrid things, leave-taking is the worst,' said he. 'Such a fortnight as it has been! Every day more precious and more delightful than the day before! – every day making me less fit to bear any other place. Happy those who can remain at Sidmouth!'

'But you will come again. This will not be your only visit?'

He made a bow in agreement. 'In short, perhaps, Miss Austen – I think you can hardly be quite without suspicion—' He looked at her, as if wanting to read her thoughts. She hardly knew what to say. It seemed like the forerunner of something absolutely serious, which she did not wish.

Forcing herself to speak, therefore, in the hope of putting it by, she said, 'You are quite in the right. Mr. Hayley and Mr. Blake demand your instant return.'

'Mr. Blake has been sorely wronged and requires my services. I am entirely at his disposal.' Rose lapsed into silence, twisting his hat in his hands. They took shelter in the Shed and observed the waves lashing the seashore.

'And Mr. Hayley. He writes a life of Mr. Cowper? Oh, I long to know more of that fine man. One cannot know another merely from reading their poetry.'

'He suffered much, Miss Austen, from the melancholy. *Hatred and vengeance, my eternal portion … Damn'd below Judas.* Oh, the pity of it. And yet, he was a man of courage and a man of profound faith.'

'God works in a mysterious way, His wonders to perform. He plants his footsteps in the sea, And rides upon the storm,' she replied softly.

'An excellent hymn!' cried Rose. 'And you are related, are you not, to his great friend, Lady Austen?'

'I am afraid not, sir, though *The Task* remains one of my favoured poems. It is in his depiction of everyday life and scenes of the English countryside that he wins my admiration. It is something that I wish to convey in my own scribblings.'

'You write verse, Miss Austen?'

'Only novels.'

'In the manner of Miss Edgeworth? If I may be so bold?'

'Indeed, sir. And Miss Burney, though my pen is much inferior to those exalted authors.'

'I will not believe it, madam. It would be the greatest privilege if …'

'My work is not for public consumption, Mr. Rose.' She turned the subject. 'Do you assist Mr. Hayley in his life of Cowper?'

'Indeed. I bring letters to Sussex for his benefit. The reason for my visit, however, is to assist Mr. Blake and to prepare his trial. He is an innocent man, incapable of treason. Now let us walk to the water's edge. The wind and rain have abated.'

As they approached the sea, Jane observed a footprint in the sand. A foamy wave splashed over and it disappeared. Her slippers began to sink into the sand, soaking her stockings and then her petticoat, and leaving Mr. Rose perturbed and worried that she might catch cold.

'My pink shoes are not particularly beautiful,' said she, brushing away his concern. 'And I am seldom ill.' She longed to hear more of Cowper and Hayley, and the abolition, but Rose insisted they return home forthwith to dry her feet. He told her he was sorry to be leaving and that he hoped to return within days.

He felt the going away almost too much to speak of it, his dejection most evident. He was silent. She believed he was looking at her; probably reflecting on what she had said and trying to understand the manner of it.

'And you will be here, when I come back to Devon?'

'Yes, until we leave for Bath. Do not look so dejected, Mr. Rose. And surely you have business to attend to in Devon upon your return.'

'My business is with you, and only with you.'

'I ought to pretend not to understand you but such false delicacy might mislead you. I make no promises, Mr. Rose. The more I know of the world, the more I am convinced that I shall never see a man whom I can really love. I require so much!' She could not help laughing. 'Excuse me,' she said, 'and be assured that I meant no offence to you by speaking in so candid a way of my own feelings.'

The sky had changed from steely grey to blue-green. The clouds were high and thin. They turned in silence. Jane's cambric handkerchief dropped from her hand onto the wet sand. He bent quickly to retrieve it and begged her to let him have it as a keepsake. At the very least, would she allow him to have it laundered before returning it? She consented with a smile.

She thought him the loneliest man she had ever met.

He could not know it, but he was looking at the only woman he would ever love, until his last, dying breath.

WEEK FIVE

Let me not to the marriage of true minds
Admit impediments.

(William Shakespeare)

Samuel Rose left for Sussex with feelings of sorrow mingled with relief. He had never met a more bewitching woman and he felt himself in acute danger. He would be glad to talk it over with Hayley. That Jane Austen was a woman worth winning, he did not doubt. It was not only her beauty and grace, but her absolute *candour* that attracted him. She was incapable of artifice, and she had unwittingly sent out a challenge when she had truthfully said that she *required so much*. Well, he flattered himself, he had much to give. He had an open heart, an affectionate disposition and wealth enough for them both. He had no family to please. His friends would be sure to admire her wit and good sense. But that he was quite frightened by the power of his feelings could not, in all truth, be denied.

Finding a wife had not been in his current scheme. He had not received enough encouragement to approach her with a firm proposal. He also feared if he did propose she would refuse him. What had she said? *I shall never see a man whom I can really love.*

At times his doubts ran strong, but at others doubts and alarms mingled with his hopes. Could she love him? Might she learn to love him? If not an outright 'no', might she be persuaded to a 'maybe'? He was quite prepared to wait for as long as it took. The smile she had bestowed upon him at their parting suggested he was not odious to her, and gave reason to hope that his addresses might not be unwelcome. All he asked was the opportunity of winning her affections. It would seem clear that without being ready to commit herself, she might be inclined to favour his suit.

He permitted such pleasing thoughts to wash over him like the incoming waves over smooth pebbles. Then he turned his mind to poor Mr. Blake and his sedition charge. He would have a fight on his hands, but he owed it to his friends, Cowper and Hayley, and had pledged to do his utmost to clear Blake's name. He must cast Miss Jane Austen from his mind, for the time being.

Rose was vastly pleased with Turret House in the Sussex village of Felpham. Hayley had built a fine marine building, with an embattled turret and an elegant library fitted out with busts and pictures, and a well laid out garden carefully enclosed with high walls for privacy's sake. The lofty turret commanded a remarkable view of the sea in one direction and the South Downs in another. In fine weather, the waves came rippling in to the gently shelving, sandy beach but when rough, with so much force as to eat away huge mouthfuls of the low, fertile coast.

Having suffered the recent deaths of his friend Cowper and his beloved son, Tom, a grief-stricken Hayley had embarked on his *Life of Cowper* and resolved that his friend Blake should engrave the illustrations for his book. He had offered William and his wife Catherine the use of a cottage by the seaward side of Felpham. Blake, when he had been introduced to Rose, was all delight and amiability.

'Our cottage looks more and more beautiful; a perfect model for cottages,' said he. 'The villagers are not mere rustics, they are polite and modest. Meat is cheaper than in London, and the sweet air and the voices of winds, trees and birds, and the odours of the happy ground, make it a dwelling for immortals. Work will go on here with God-speed.'

Blake's cottage was a long, shallow, white-faced house of three rooms on the ground floor and three above, with a thatched roof and a verandah running the length of the house. There was a slip of garden in front, enclosed by a low flint wall. In front again was a private way shaded by evergreens and ample gardens. Beyond, a cornfield stretched to the sea. Further seawards stood two wind-mills turning conspicuously on a tongue of land that shut off the adjacent Bognor from sight. A few steps up the winding lane by the Old Fox Inn brought Blake to the postern-like gate of his patron's house in the centre of the village.

Hayley was an agreeable companion: kind-hearted and generous, constantly on the alert to advance Blake's fortunes; the recent charges against his friend had caused him much distress.

'It's a trumped-up charge, Samuel,' said he. 'Entirely the ruse of a drunken, disgraced soldier. No oath was made about the King.'

'Then we must discover reliable witnesses, William. It seems clear to me the whole business is a fabricated perjury. A contemptible business, and should never have been brought to the bench. Now that he has found bail, he is bound over to make an appearance at Chichester quarter-sessions during Michaelmas. But presently there is much to be done.' Rose took out his pocket watch as if to make his point more strongly.

'He has been very much degraded and injuriously treated, and his wife has been half-terrified to death by a charge of *high treason* against her husband.'

Blake had remained silent throughout this exchange. He was short and pale, dressed in threadbare clothes. His grey britches were shiny at the front through wear. He had a soft, round face and large eyes. He had just returned from a long walk across open countryside, where, so Blake said, he had got into an argument with a thistle. He told Rose about his visions: Moses and the Prophets, Homer, Dante, Milton. 'All majestic shadows, grey but luminous and superior to all common height of men.'

He had the unmistakable accent of a lifelong Londoner.

Rose thought him mesmerising, like a meteor. He was all imagination.

'Did you ever see a fairy's funeral?' asked Blake.

'Never, sir,' said Samuel.

'I have, but not before last night. I was walking alone in my garden; there was a great stillness among the branches and flowers, and more than common sweetness in the air. I heard a low and pleasant sound, and I know not whence it came. At last I saw the broad leaf of a flower move and underneath I saw a procession of creatures of the size and colour of green and grey grasshoppers, bearing a body laid out on a rose leaf, which they buried with songs, and then disappeared. It was a fairy funeral!'

Blake showed Rose his engraving of Michelangelo: a full-length portrait of the great Florentine looking out on the world with a searching gaze, the Colosseum in the background. He had recently engaged in miniature-painting.

'Miniature has become a goddess in my eyes,' said he to Rose, 'and my friends in Sussex say that I excel in the pursuit. I have a great many orders, and they multiply.'

He offered to paint a miniature of Samuel Rose, admiring his sure countenance, aquiline nose and cornflower blue eyes. Rose agreed to sit for him, anxious to hear more of Blake's conversation, so unlike any other. Momentarily, all thoughts of Jane Austen were expunged from his mind. Until it occurred to him that he could keep the miniature for her, if he could only persuade her to accept it.

The carriage approached Wokefield Park via a canopy of ancient oaks, their branches forming a stately avenue befitting the dignity of the house to which they led. Reverend Swete, seated opposite his young charge, cast frequent glances at her solemn face, which betrayed neither excitement nor fear but rather the deep reserve of a child who had long since learned to guard her feelings. Little Leah sat with her hands folded in her lap, her small frame barely filling the corner of the seat, but her dark, watchful eyes missed nothing of their surroundings.

As the carriage drew to a halt before the grand portico, the door was opened by a footman, and Lady Sarah Brocas herself descended the steps to greet them. She was a woman of striking presence, her complexion a warm, rich brown that seemed to glow in the sunlight. Her countenance was adorned with a gracious smile, which she extended first to Reverend Swete and then, with equal sincerity, to Leah.

'Reverend Swete,' she said, holding out her hand, 'it is a pleasure to make your acquaintance. And this,' she added, stooping to bring herself to the child's eye level, 'must be Miss Leah. You are most welcome to Wokefield, my dear.'

Leah clung to her grandfather's hand and said nothing, though her wide eyes took in every detail of Lady Brocas's face and elegant dress.

'The child must be exhausted from such a long journey,' said Lady Brocas, gesturing to a maid, who took Leah by the hand and led her into the house, where she could be washed and given a change of clothing.

'Lady Brocas,' Reverend Swete began, his voice trembling with gratitude, 'your generosity in receiving us cannot be overstated. My granddaughter has seen much sorrow in her short life. To know that she will be under your care is a comfort beyond measure.'

Lady Brocas straightened and smiled. 'I shall endeavour to make her feel at home, Reverend. Your gratitude is also due to our mutual friend, Miss Jane Austen. Come inside; we can discuss the arrangements at leisure.'

Their conversation resumed in the library.

'I am of the firm belief, your Ladyship, that my wife will soon relent, and forgive our son, whereupon she will open the doors of Oxton House to his child.'

Lady Brocas was not so sanguine.

'My dear sir,' said she, 'prejudices imbibed in the nursery are frequently attached to the beings of ripened years, and to eradicate them as they appear is a labour well worth the endeavour of the judicious preceptor. Perhaps it is a little late in the day for your good lady to overcome her enmity. Let us trust the child will meet with liberality and munificence elsewhere in this island.'

He bowed his thanks. His tone was subdued. 'To be educated as a lady is my son's dearest wish for her, in order to qualify her to enjoy the privileges and immunities of the white women of this country, and to render her useful to society. She has been met with much hostility on her own native shores, and my son observes that education there is at the lowest ebb. To talk of a *Homer*, or a *Virgil*, or a *Demosthenes*, is quite unpolite. He will not think of sending her to school in the Americas, or Scotland. Nor even Miss Bennett in Savannah-la-Mar.'

'Miss Bennett is a worthy woman,' replied Lady Brocas, 'to whom my own father sent me to gain a little learning before he consigned my brothers and me to England to avail ourselves of an education unavailable in the West Indies. Your son is to be commended for his desire that his *daughter* be educated within these isles.'

Understanding all too well the complexities of Miss Leah's position in society, she was ready to consider the child as her own. She would instruct her mantua-maker to line a silk spencer with fur and work another in light wool for day use. She had fretted about the delicate health of the girl, fearing the ill reports of the 'muslin disease' then sweeping France. Little wonder in this frigid climate, she had remarked, that fine ladies in their wispy muslin sheaths were freezing to death. Her husband, Sir Bernard, had responded drily that there was no cause for worry, England was enjoying a most temperate summer. Perhaps he was right. At first sight, the child appeared *quite robust*, the picture of health. Nevertheless, she should be fed asses' milk from the dairy, beef tea and calf-foot jellies as befitting an invalid.

Inviting the Reverend Swete to take some refreshment before his return journey, Lady Brocas swept purposefully out of the library.

'Poor, motherless child,' said she to no one in particular. She thought of her own mother, who had been despatched to Manchester following the death of her father. Bought for ninety pounds, she had produced three fine babies and had lived with Mr. Redhead until the time of his death. Mrs. Bullock, as she was known, was now mistress of a boarding house in the North of England, devoting herself chiefly to her second son, George, who had entered the militia after Cambridge.

Lady Brocas ascended the grand staircase and then the back stairs to the room that had been prepared for Miss Swete.

Leah, dressed in a fresh white pinafore, was sitting on the edge of the bed, gazing at a glass bowl that had been placed on the bedside table.

'And what is this you have brought with you, my dear?'

Lady Brocas leaned forward to inspect the goldfish, which swam in slow, graceful circles in its watery prison. 'How charming! Does it have a name, I wonder?'

For a moment there was no response, but then a small voice broke the silence. 'His name is Star,' Leah said, her words barely above a whisper but clear nonetheless.

'Star! What a lovely name,' Lady Brocas said gently. 'And does Star remind you of something, my dear? Perhaps the sea?'

Leah nodded, her small hand reaching instinctively towards the bowl as if to reassure herself of its presence. 'He is like the stars in the water,' she murmured, her voice gaining a little more strength.

Lady Brocas's smile deepened. 'How poetic you are, Miss Leah. I daresay we shall have many such lovely thoughts from you in the days to come. But now we must bid farewell to your grandfather.'

She led the child downstairs, where she told the Reverend Swete that Leah had introduced her to Star. Overcome with astonishment, he reached out to place a hand on Leah's shoulder. 'You see, my dear,' he said quietly, 'you are already finding your voice. Lady Brocas will guide you further, and in time, I am sure, you will flourish.'

The conversation turned then to more practical matters, with Lady Brocas outlining her plans for Leah's education. 'I have found an excellent governess and I will instruct her in the art of watercolour myself. And I should like to introduce her gradually to the society of the neighbourhood, for I know, as you do, Reverend, how important it is that she be accustomed to the company of others.'

Reverend Swete nodded, though his expression was tinged with melancholy. 'You have thought of everything, Lady Brocas. I am confident that under your care, she will become all that her father dreamed she might be.'

When the moment of parting arrived, Leah clung to her grandfather with an intensity that brought tears to his eyes. 'You must be brave, my little one,' he said, his voice faltering. 'You are in the best of hands, and I shall visit you as often as I am able.'

Lady Brocas stepped forward, her presence steady and reassuring. 'We shall take very good care of her, Reverend Swete. You may rest easy on that account.'

With one final embrace, the reverend departed, his heart heavy with sorrow yet also lifted by hope. As the carriage rolled away, he cast one last look at Wokefield Park, its noble façade glowing in the golden light of the afternoon. He whispered a silent prayer for the child he had left behind.

That evening, Lady Sarah Brocas dismissed her house-maid, Lucy, and untangled Leah's curly hair first with her hands and then with a tortoiseshell comb. She talked to her of Antigua, as much for her own sake as for the child's, its pink-white sands, its turquoise ocean, the lush tamarind trees. She did not speak of her home in Betty's Hope, nor its ever-twirling twin windmills and the sweet sickly smell of molasses that filled the air.

Lonely in her mansion, and longing for children of her own, Lady Sarah had found a charming companion in this amiable child entrusted to her care.

The days slipped by, with no sign of Mr. Rose. Jane took solace in her scribbling, whenever there was a spare moment. Writing as though her life depended on it.

'Do you miss your friend greatly?' said Cassie.

'I never expected to see Mr. Rose again,' she replied stoically. 'My sole consolation is that I had never given him any cause to suspect the impression he had made upon me.'

'Time will generally lessen the interest of every attachment not within the daily circle, my dear Jane,' said Cassie soothingly. 'His not pressing you for an answer is a proof of good sense, and he has risen even more in my good graces.'

'How quick come the reasons for approving what we like.' Her beautiful hazel eyes were fixed on her sister. 'One cannot help the way the wind blows, but one can direct the sails.'

Privately, Jane *had* missed him. She had given him reason to hope that his addresses might not be unwelcome and she had expected him to return to Devonshire. The warm air made it difficult to sleep at night and she had found herself remembering their final meeting. She had grown used to seeing him, she could not deny.

Towards the end of the week, the Reverend Swete returned from Wokefield. He was quick to make his way to Dove Lane, where he had become a firm favourite of George Austen. The gentlemen discussed the news of the day, the beauties of Sidmouth and George's unceasing interest in the exploits of his sailor sons. The Battle of Algeciras was much on Mr. Austen's mind, though the latest intelligence had brought good news. Frank's younger brother, Charles, somewhat in the elder's shadow, had made his family proud by a recent daring venture. He had set off in a small boat, in a gale, with only four other men, and succeeded in boarding and taking possession of the eighteen-gun *Scipio*, with one hundred and forty-nine men aboard.

'Oh, what a delight to be the begetter of such intrepid young men,' said the reverend, with a sigh. He thought of his eldest son, with all his wealth and connections, and how he had squandered his opportunities.

'My boys must fend for themselves,' said Mrs. Austen, interrupting the conversation. 'It has long been my creed that a life of early hardship and discipline must be an advantage to those without a fortune of their own.'

Jane, who was writing a letter to Frank, felt a stab of guilt, as she had this moment commissioned her brother for the purchase of two Indian muslin shawls.

'How does Miss Swete do?' said she, putting down her pen.

The girl's grandpapa, grateful for Jane's intervention, both now and in her former application to Wokefield on his behalf, reverted happily to the subject of the child's improvement. The change of scene had worked an instant wonder: she had already begun to speak.

'How unexpected! Such happiness must be yours,' said Jane, 'and what precipitated this momentous event? Did she say "yes, please, ma'am" upon being offered a whipped syllabub?'

'Lady Brocas informed me that the agent of the miracle was Mr. Rose's goldfish.'

Jane was reduced to silence.

'And what news of Mr. Rose himself?' enquired her father. Jane was grateful for his question, as she had longed to ask it herself.

'I am glad that you asked,' said Reverend Swete. 'He has been a most admirable addition to our happy few, our band of brothers and sisters here by the sea, has he not, Miss Jane? By chance, I mentioned his name when I was writing to a clergy acquaintance of mine in Sussex and upon my return from Wokefield Park I found his reply, in which he gave a full account of Rose's remarkable career in the law.'

'Pray, tell,' said Jane, her interest piqued.
He handed her the letter.

His first opportunity of displaying professional ability occurred in Chichester, where, having a clergyman for his client, he conciliated the esteem of his audience by expatiating with propriety, eloquence, and success, on the character of a divine. He was still more admired for the display of a talent peculiarly striking in a barrister of no experience: in questioning a good, but misguided woman, he showed not only a decent, but a most delicate indulgence to her sex and situation, yet ingeniously and tenderly drew from her all the information that was sufficient to establish the innocence of his client.

Swete's friend, it occurred to Jane, had a style as prolix as that of the reverend himself. She smiled to herself in such a way that she was ill-prepared for what came next.

Though, like most men of middling stature, he possesses a considerable portion of bodily strength and agility, his constitution is naturally fragile. Soon after he began to exercise his profession, his friends were apprehensive that his progress in it might be cruelly impeded by the appearance of hereditary gout. On a circumstance so alarming it

was suggested to him that perhaps his best mode of
guarding against the evils that might arise from an
enemy so insidious and formidable would be to
make an early retreat from the very laborious
profession of the law, and take refuge in the
honourable tranquillity of the church. The idea
engaged his serious deliberation, because a
nobleman of singular beneficence, who knew his
merits, and his critical situation, most liberally
offered to him the refuge in question by a
conditional promise of ecclesiastical preferment.

So he is indeed most sincere in his faith, thought Jane, with satisfaction. She was, however, rendered uneasy by this intelligence of his uncertain health.

She handed back the letter.

'The spirit of Rose,' explained the indefatigable Swete, 'was deeply affected by this unexpected offer of patronage, and as his exemplary father had early impressed on his mind the belief of Christianity, he was far from feeling any motives of conscience that could make him unwilling to become a minister of the religion which he revered. But he had ever entertained a high sense of personal honour, which would be offended by such a change of course.'

Jane's fears were exacerbated when the reverend reported the news that Rose was, it seemed, at this moment unwell – much indisposed with a bad cold caught on his way to the county sessions – nothing serious – summer colds were prevalent this season – Sussex sea air not so sweet as Sidmouth – such a fine open sea.

'How sorry I am,' said she. 'But he will soon recover. He is a robust gentleman.'

'He is an *honourable* gentleman, and Mr. Blake is most grateful to him for serving his cause so well. He has been sorely wronged and Mr. Rose is the only lawyer in the land who will accept his case. He refuses to accept a penny from Mr. Blake. He considers him to be a great genius, to be cherished and protected. But Mr. Rose works untiringly on his friend's behalf. He must learn to guard his strength.'

Jane and her father nodded their agreement.

'The value of good health,' said Mr. Austen, 'is only really apparent to those who have been seriously ill.'

Her father's observation made Jane reflect upon her own illness in Southampton – a dirty place – when she was a young girl at school. The typhus, brought from the soldiers in the barracks, had raged through the town. She had drawn upon her will, fighting to live. Only when she was brought home to Steventon had she begun to recover. She could remember the great peace and calm that flowed into her like a flood of warm light and renewed her strength. Her brush with death had reinforced her spirit and her vitality.

That health was the most precious of blessings was brought home when her mother, a lady of resolute constitution but troubled often by the caprices of her valetudinarian sensibility, complained that the seaside air had been insufficient to restore her spirits and that she was in need of a visit from the celebrated Dr. Russell.

He duly arrived the following day, carrying with him a small jar covered with a muslin cloth. The contents were both familiar and formidable. With a countenance of practised serenity, he informed Mrs. Austen that a course of leeches was, in his professional opinion, the most appropriate remedy for her present malady. Though the good lady was not unacquainted with the treatment, she could not entirely suppress a shudder at the thought of the cold, clammy creatures that were soon to be affixed to her person. Yet she bore the prospect with a stoic grace.

The physician, ever meticulous in his preparations, took out two of the wriggling creatures and placed them on Mrs. Austen's arms. Guided by some instinct known only to themselves, they immediately sought a place where they might begin their sanguineous work. The sensation, at first, was that of an unpleasant tugging, as the leeches fastened themselves securely to the skin. Mrs. Austen turned her gaze to the window, finding solace in the sight of a seagull suspended in the air, while the lowly creatures continued their duty in companionable silence. As the minutes passed, the leeches swelled with the richness of the blood they drew until Dr. Russell, satisfied with the progress, removed the bloated wrigglers and dropped them back into his jar, to rest there until called upon again.

He assured a now faint Mrs. Austen that the treatment had been successful and that she would soon feel the benefit of the slight depletion of her humours. With a weak but grateful smile, she thanked the doctor and resolved to take a restorative green tea, confident that her health, though so precarious, would soon be restored to its usual, if fragile, state.

That evening, Jane and Cassie strolled to the sea, arm in arm. The moon hung low over the wine-dark cliffs and had turned from copper to silver. The stars were bright and the air velvet-soft. Jane whispered:

'I am constant as the northern star
Of whose true-fixed and resting quality
There is no fellow in the firmament.'

'Next time I have the happiness to see you, I am determined to paint another portrait of you from life in my best manner, for memory will not do in such minor operations; for I have now discovered that without nature before the painter's eye, he can never produce anything in the walks of natural painting. Historical designing is one thing, and portrait-painting another, and they are as distinct as any two arts can be. Happy would that man be who could unite them.'

Blake was satisfied with his miniature portrait of Samuel Rose. The latter had it set in plain gold with no embellishments, while he recovered from his bad cold. Catherine Blake had nursed him well. Rose had been moved by the union. Mr. and Mrs. Blake had been married for seventeen years and were as fond of each other as if their Honey Moon were still shining. She could draw and engrave, and sing delightfully, and was so truly the half of her good man that the two seemed animated by one soul.

Rose bade farewell to Felpham, pleased with the preparations he had made for the trial. During his stay, he had won a large share of the poet's regard and favour. His exertions had been great.

Blake's gratitude overflowed, and his miniature water-colour on ivory showed to effect the noble mien and fine countenance of the young lawyer. Rose held it in his hands, tracing his finger over its smooth finish. He wondered if she, for whom it had been painted, would be gratified with the results. He wondered indeed if she would ever see the miniature, would trace *her* finger over the ivory oval. Perhaps touch it with her lips. He was thinner and paler than when he had first arrived in Sussex, but the eyes glittered as brightly as ever. He slipped the portrait into its velvet-lined case. Perhaps it was time to return to London, he thought, where he belonged.

No, he did not mean to return. Of that she felt sure.

They were approaching their final week in Sidmouth. The lodgings in Sydney Place were finally furnished and ready for use. She heartily despised Bath, but what could she, a mere woman, do? She walked to the edge of the sea, the water foamy and tinged with pink, like blood. She turned away and it was then that she saw him. A tall figure walking quickly, now running towards her. There was nobody else on the vast yellow sands, just the glittering sea and the hard bright sun overhead.

WEEK SIX

O Rose thou art sick

(William Blake)

'Do not you think, Mr. Austen, that the last century has quietly taken its last breath. Is not the year eighteen hundred and one a time of radical adjustment?' Mr. Rose, more content than he had been for many years, looked up from his newspaper.

'My son, Frank, is not so confident, Mr. Rose. It continues to be a profitable business, with more trade than ever crossing the Atlantic. But perhaps there are other considerations that add to your present good cheer? My daughter will arrive presently. She and her sister have taken their last dip. It may be some time before we return to the sea.'

Rose smiled his beatific smile. 'And you proceed to Colyton in a few days, sir? Might I seek your permission to follow you there when I have resolved some matters here in Devonshire?'

George Austen gave his acquiescence with a bow. Samuel Rose took out his handkerchief. 'And you might see a surgeon about that cough, my dear sir.'

'It is nothing, merely a cold I caught in Sussex. I will bathe today and take the waters.'

'I shall ring the bell for Mrs. Austen. Dr. Turton's receipt for a cold is as good a remedy as you will find among any of the fine medical men in Sidmouth.'

'Pray do not trouble Mrs. Austen. And here are her daughters refreshed from Mrs. Molly's administrations. How do you do, Miss Austen, Miss Jane?'

The girls came in with a great bustle, laughter ringing in the air. They took off their bonnets and hung them on the rack.

'Papa, it was bracingly cold. How do you do, Mr. Rose.' Cassie was the first to speak.

'Chocolate, the girls require chocolate. Warms the marrow, don't you think, Mr. Rose?' This time he did ring the bell.

Jane's eyes sparkled and danced, and her complexion was pink and rosy. Her father observed to himself that his daughter's admiration for Mr. Rose had softened her hard edges. Mrs. Austen bustled into the parlour with a tray of chocolate. 'Do come and sit by the fire, girls. You'll catch your death of cold.'

'Mama, it's excessively warm this morning,' said Jane. Nevertheless, she accepted Mr. Rose's offer of a shawl, which he placed around her shoulders. He took out his watch and with an anxious glance took his leave, mumbling something about an urgent appointment – though not before the lovers had arranged a promenade along the Mall for later that day.

'What on earth is his hurry?' said Jane in amazement. The girls sat and sipped their chocolate. It did indeed warm the bones. Mrs. Austen was red in the cheeks and beads of perspiration bubbled on her forehead.

'Girls, make haste. As soon as you are warmed through, you must finish your packing. Your father has written to Richard at Colyton. He expects us by Thursday. We will sojourn with him for a few days on our way to Bath. We must not delay. Jane, there is a letter from Frank at Spithead. I think yours has crossed in the post.'

'Mama, it is only Monday. And you promised a visit to Mr. Hall's to see the lace.' She did not want to think about the time she had left.

'It will be such a pleasure to see dear Richard again,' said Cassie. He had been a pupil at Steventon, had taken orders after Oxford and was ensconced in east Devonshire with a wife.

'What news of Frank, dear?' said Mrs. Austen. 'Still at Portsmouth waiting for the wind to change, I expect?' Jane was silent as she perused the letter, until she exclaimed.

'Mama, Frank is made. He was yesterday raised to the rank of flag captain of the *Neptune*. What glorious news. And, before you dry your tears of joy, he has more news of brother Charles. His latest voyage to Lisbon was in the service of Prince Augustus. He suffers from the asthma, so Charles says, and required the warmer climate. They were very well pleased with their royal guest, whom they found fat, jolly and affable. How like Charles to say so!'

'And the *Neptune* a ninety-eight gun, my dear?'

'Indeed, Papa.'

'What a happy day. On the strength of this good fortune, perhaps we shall buy new muslin gowns from Mr. Hall's. We must not delay, Cassie.'

'A capital idea,' said Mrs. Austen. 'Your father shall provide you with a draft for the amount of it.'

It could do no harm, and perhaps would do a great deal of good, for Jane to be seen in a new gown. Mrs. Austen was excessively pleased with her daughter's new-found contentment. Jane had never looked so well, nor in such good health. Sidmouth had been a blessing to them. Dear Sidmouth! A wave of relief washed over her, as she contemplated her daughter's fortune. Sussex was not so very far away, and they would have a house in London, close to brother Henry and Eliza. There was no engagement as yet, but all the circumstances and proofs of affection led her to believe that Mr. Rose considered Jane his future wife.

Lady Brocas surveyed her domain with satisfaction. Sir John Soane had made his final improvements to Wokefield, the landscaped gardens, the rows of flower beds, estimated to be the best in England. But nothing pleased her more than the gateway with the double crest of her African ancestors. Her husband had expressed an interest in removing to Beaurepaire, the family's other estate in Hampshire, but she could not bear to leave the gates. She had much on her mind that morning, having received a letter from her brother, Henry.

He had been tried on charges of conspiracy and now languished in Dorchester gaol. Having spent all of his large inheritance from their father, he was appealing to his sister for money. It really was too tiresome. Since leaving Cambridge, he had been in trouble in one way or another, never wanting to settle down in any place. One minute writing an abolitionist tract and the next recanting his position. Her elder brother, Joseph, a surgeon, was an altogether more reliable gentleman.

Lady Brocas had decided not to inform her husband about Henry's problems. She had plentiful wealth of her own and still owned property in the West Indies. Her father had insisted in his bequest that the Antiguan property was solely for her, and not for any future husband who should intermeddle with it. She would consult with her lawyers and have the bail money sent.

She glanced fondly at Leah, who was standing at her side, staring at the gateway. The girl was speaking fluently and had even begun to call her Mama. Lady Brocas took comfort in her ministrations. She had only been wed for one year and yet she had thrown herself into mothering with aplomb. Leah was a darling child, but her appetite was small, and the lady feared for smallpox.

They turned back to the house to greet William Swete, who had arrived the previous evening to see how his daughter was settling in her new home. Having introduced him to Leah's governess and dispatched teacher and pupil to the schoolroom, they discussed the girl's progress. William acknowledged that Lady Brocas was living, breathing proof that a woman of colour could take her rightful place in English society, but explained that as a precaution, he had manumitted his daughter and provided for her handsomely in his will.

'Do you consider the child returning to the West Indies, Mr. Swete?'

'I do not, madam,' said he. 'It will be no secret to you that, despite my mother's prejudice, my daughter will have more friends here than in Antigua. The natural offspring of my slave can never be considered in the light of equality by the English planters. Such is the wretched state of degradation to which my unhappy fellow creatures are sunk in the western hemisphere.'

'You loved the child's mother, Mr. Swete. And yet your own prejudices forbade you to make her your wife?' He accepted the charge without demur. He felt all the justice of the reproof.

'The seducer of innocence is always guilty, madam. The difference of climate or colour makes no difference to the crime. Elizabeth paid the ultimate price, but I will see that her daughter does not suffer.'

Lady Brocas reflected, with a stab of sympathy, on the wives of the English planters, forced to endure the presence of their husband's illegitimate children in their homes. Unable to face the facts of their existence or unwilling to do so.

'How does your mother do, sir?'

'Your patronage, Lady Brocas, has been the instigator of a weak amelioration of her illiberal prejudices. But I cannot pretend to believe that the leopard changes its spots.'

'I see. Well, we shall not trespass on your time more than is necessary, Mr. Swete. The child is welcome at Wokefield for as long as you require.'

There was one more question. The matter of the smallpox variolation. Lady Brocas had a suspicion that he would not hear of inoculation, foolish man, fearing what he did not understand. But she was well-prepared.

'Pray do not believe that such methods are revolutionary, Mr. Swete, or confined to the efforts of Dr. Jenner and his dairy maids. My brethren have practised the art of variolation for centuries. I myself was variolated by my nurse when a child, at my father's behest. We are not savages, you know.'

'Children from the West Indies are vulnerable in health, madam. I fear for my daughter and hear of children dying from the procedure. This is a risk I cannot take.'

'Nonsense, Mr. Swete. You are misinformed. Despite what the newspapers write, children from Africa are no more delicate or sickly than any other child born of English soil. Miss Jane Austen, to whom we owe so much in regard to Leah, has informed me by letter that she and all her brothers and sisters were inoculated at the hands of Madame Lefroy in Hampshire and escaped the plague. The Miss Lloyds were *not*, and their pock-marked complexions are testament to their mother's neglect.'

This intelligence was enough to make him afraid. 'Then I give my consent, Lady Brocas, provided you take her to Madam Lefroy.'

'It can certainly be arranged the next time we travel to Beaurepaire. I would suggest that we do not delay.'

He was dismissed, and Lady Brocas walked to the bow window, beyond which the green plantations stretched for miles towards the ha-ha. The fine weather had changed and a fierce rain lashed the windows. The gentleman was doing his utmost to right his wrongs, she considered. But he could never know what the child had suffered, and would continue to suffer, displaced from her native country, ripped from her mother and forced to endure the stares of her father's family.

Sarah Redhead was now the lady of the manor and yet her own beloved mother, mistress of a boarding house in Manchester, was unwelcome at Wokefield. That much her husband had made clear. The prejudice of Mrs. John Swete was explicit and she did little to hide her antipathy. It was altogether a different matter for those who concealed their judgement behind a carapace of good breeding.

This painful intelligence only increased the bonds between Lady Brocas and the child with every passing day. She would keep her at Wokefield for as long as she could. The thought of parting from her was now unendurable.

'Shall I read you a poem, Mr. Rose?' He nodded in acquiescence. She gave him the sweetest of smiles as she cleared her throat, choosing 'The Rose' by William Cowper. 'The rose had been washed, just washed in a shower,' she began, her voice melodious:

'Which Mary to Anna conveyed;
The plentiful moisture encumbered the flower,
And weighed down its beautiful head.

I hastily seized it, unfit as it was
For a nosegay, so dripping and drowned,
And swinging it rudely, too rudely, alas!
I snapped it; it fell to the ground.

And such, I exclaimed, is the pitiless part
Some act by the delicate mind,
Regardless of wringing and breaking a heart
Already to sorrow resigned.

This elegant rose, had I shaken it less,
Might have bloomed with its owner awhile;
And the tear that is wiped with a little address,
May be followed perhaps by a smile.'

'Brava, Miss Austen,' said he, clapping his hands. 'Now pray tell me the meaning of this delightful verse. I bow to your superior knowledge and taste.'

'It is about the fragile nature of the heart, Mr. Rose, and the consequences of insensitivity. The poor broken rose, so hastily plucked from the rosebush, is as the pain of the heart suffering from neglect.'

'And more than that, perhaps, Cowper's rose is an allegory for the "delicate mind"? He wishes us to treat his tender feelings and sensibility with care, and understanding, does he not?'

Rose thought of his friend, and his attempts at self-annihilation. How to comprehend despair when his own life was flooded with happiness. He wondered how he could bear to be parted from her, though his intention to see the family again as soon as they returned to Sydney Place had been welcomed enthusiastically. It would be a mercifully short separation, little more than the duration of the trial. He took out his watch. How the minutes raced by when they were together. If only he could stop time.

Cassie walked into the parlour. She had been packing her trunk. 'Good morning, Mr. Rose,' said she with a bright smile. 'I hear we are to meet in east Devonshire.'

'I shall be leaving Hook's Hotel in a fortnight,' he replied. 'And I shall make my way to you.' Cassie observed that he had not shaken off his cough. 'Do you see your physician, Mr. Rose? We have the very best here at Sidmouth, do we not?'

'Dr. Russell is the best of men, indeed,' he replied. '"The Sea Washes Away all the Evils of Mankind." I do confess, half a pint of seawater is a little more than I can stomach. Do we not have the saltiest water along the coast? The good doctor plans to have me massaged with fresh seaweed.' The sisters burst out laughing.

Cassie looked at him with approval. He was the only gentleman she had ever seen whom she felt worthy of her sister. He was good and he was noble. His kindness towards the poet Blake, his attention to Miss Swete and his discretion in the case of Captain Parker proclaimed him to be a gentleman of sense and compassion. He seemed incapable of artifice or affectation. His only fault, if it could be called a fault, was a similarity in taste, which so perfectly coincided with her sister's. They shared the same feelings about books, music and painting. His passion for the cause of the abolitionists could only be matched by Jane's own fervour.

Samuel Rose's greatest desire was for Jane to read from her manuscripts. This she rejected outright. She was never quite satisfied in her writing and, with the exception of Martha, refused to share her stories with anyone outside of the family.

'But how *do* you write when you are away from home?' he asked.

'Without the slightest difficulty,' interjected Cassie fondly. 'She picks up her pen and scribbles away, laughing to herself as she goes. If she is disturbed by visitors, she locks her paper away in her box. She is determined that nobody should know of her hobby-horse. She's been that way since a girl. My father believes she has a rare talent and writes in a manner entirely new. We think it too.'

'I abhor false modesty, so I shall agree with everything you say and disagree with nothing,' said Jane with a laugh. 'But I am not to be persuaded out of my inclinations, Mr. Rose. You shall have to be patient. Though it is by no means a foregone conclusion that my novels shall ever see the light of day.'

With that he was forced to be content. I shall build her a library, he thought with a start. Where she shall not be disturbed by visitors, nor even by her husband or her children. As a wedding present, he would fill the shelves with handsome editions of her favourite works. Cowper would, of course, take pride of place alongside Shakespeare. And there would be a copy of Miss Edgeworth's *Belinda*, the novel that united them during their early days of discord. He made a silent prayer of gratitude for circulating libraries.

As he took his leave, indulging these most pleasant of thoughts, he begged her to accept the miniature painted by William Blake. She was taken by surprise, and meant to refuse, but he pressed the picture into her hand with a look of such earnest devotion that made it impossible. It was Blake's workmanship and talent that were of interest, he said. His flushed complexion and brightness of eyes made him, momentarily, appear otherworldly. As he walked out of the door, and into the driving rain, she observed the hunch of his broad shoulders, which suddenly, and inexplicably, caught at her heart.

The trunks were packed and they had enjoyed a final breakfast. Mr. Rose and Miss Jane had arranged for a walk on the Mall. She was wearing the same lace veil as when he had first set eyes upon her, its texture as fine as a spider's web. He felt at one with the sunlight and the warmth of a perfect summer's day. He seemed overpowered by the kindness with which she received him.

They spoke of Miss Swete.

'Lady Brocas has written to tell me that she will not part with her and as the child will not part with Lady Brocas, she will remain in Berkshire while her father returns to Antigua to oversee his business. Mrs. John Swete saves face, wretched woman, and the Reverend is optimistic that all shall be well. *Omnia bene erunt!*'

He chuckled. They walked to the water's edge, the ocean pinker than usual following the summer squall. 'Like a sea of blood,' said he.

'When you do dance, I wish you
A wave o' th' sea, that you might every do
Nothing but that, move still, still so,
And own no other function. Each your doing,
So singular in each particular,
Crowns what you are doing in the present deeds,
That all your acts are queens.

'Shakespeare has something for every occasion, does he not?'

'Indeed,' she replied. 'He is a great favourite with my family. We all talk Shakespeare, use his similes and describe with his descriptions.'

'Yes, Shakespeare one gets acquainted with without knowing how. It is part of an Englishman's constitution. His thoughts and beauties are so spread abroad that one touches them everywhere, one is intimate with him by instinct. No man of any brain can open at a good part of one of his plays without falling into the flow of his meaning immediately.'

'That is an apt description, Mr. Rose, admirably put. Perhaps also an Englishwoman's constitution?'

He bowed his acquiescence.

'His women are flesh and blood, are they not, Miss Austen? Equal to men in courage and intelligence.'

'Certainly. And in wit,' said she, thinking of her favourite lively ladies, Beatrice and Rosalind. 'In Shakespeare's women, wit is the salt of conversation, not the food.'

'One of the many advantages of Bath is its Theatre Royal,' said he. 'The magnificent Mr. Elliston!'

'My mother is an admirer of Mr. Cooke.'

'Ah, yes, a great actor, especially when he is sober. And what of the women? Mrs. Siddons I admire greatly, but none so much as Mrs. Jordan. Her Rosalind is so very natural, yet it is not as an actress but as herself that she charms everyone. She is inimitable in all her characters because there is no one else like her.'

'It is a pity we have not finished *As You Like It* – we will put it by for when you come again.'

He was silent and grave at the thought of her departure. He coughed and took out the handkerchief she had given him.

'Miss Austen, will you grant me permission to write to you?' She agreed, with a shy smile. She was a beguiling combination of reserve and vivacity, and, as such, irresistible to him. There was no time to delay and he was powerless to prevent the swell of emotion that overcame him. He had tears in his pale blue eyes as he spoke.

'You are too good to trifle with my feelings. You can be in no doubt that you are the only woman I could ever love. As to describing the extreme wish I have for you to learn to love me – it is in vain to attempt it. If I could but succeed in giving you an idea of what it is to respect and admire you and love with one's whole heart a person whose warm affection one is sure of possessing and with whom one is assuredly to spend one's future life in the most intimate, the most sacred of all connections.'

She was astonished, temporarily, by the violence of his emotion, his equable manners suspended in the heat and agitation of the moment. But, oh, what a thing to win the affections of such a man! She was so overcome with feelings of happiness and surety that no words were necessary. Encouraged by her demeanour of tenderness and gratitude, he took her gloved hand, with its elegant, tapering fingers, and raised it to his lips.

The look she bestowed upon him was all the assurance he required. There was perfect amity between them. She desired only a little less haste. After all, they had all the time in the world, stretching before them like the endless golden sands of Sidmouth.

'Write to me, Mr. Rose.'

'It is more than I can hope for. God bless you.'

There was no time for explanation in the bustle of the departure to Colyton. Cassie searched her sister's face, which remained inscrutable throughout the journey. On arrival, Mr. Austen was especially delighted to be reunited with his old pupil Richard Buller, and to meet his new wife, Anna.

The newly-weds radiated contentment, welcoming the family into Brcrcwood House, a pleasant vicarage set in a stone-built village close to the church of St Andrews and overlooking the River Coly. News was exchanged. Richard expressed his happiness that the Austens were to be settled in Bath. Jane observed her parents' cheerfulness as they contemplated retirement in the city where they had met and been married. Now she had her own reasons for anticipating the brightest of futures, the only stain on her happiness the thought of leaving behind her sister. The very idea was unendurable.

After a hearty supper of white soup, mutton and apple pie, the girls were shown to their bedchamber, where they were finally at leisure to speak.

'Mrs. Buller is a pleasant woman. Sensible and warm-hearted. Do not you think so, Jane?'

'He is most deserving of her. And she of him. I was afraid he would oppress me with his felicity and love for his wife, but this is not the case. He calls her simply *Anna* without any angelic embellishments, for which I respect and wish him happy. She has that quiet composedness of mind which always seems sufficient to itself.'

Cassie smiled. Jane appeared restored to her good humour, though there was a thoughtfulness in her eyes. She put on her cap and put out the candle. The dark, still night enveloped them, the moon silvery bright through the casement window.

'Mrs. Buller is uncommonly large,' Cassie whispered. 'Her situation is not an enviable one. Her baby will be born at Christmas, she is certain.'

'Poor animal. I do pity her. Nothing shortens a woman's days so much as being married when too young. She will be worn out before she is thirty.'

'Our sister Elizabeth is in that way again.'

'How can she honestly be breeding again? I would recommend to her and our brother the simple regimen of separate bedrooms.'

Cassie laughed at the remark.

'And what of Samuel Rose, Jane? You have said nothing of your meeting. Mama has concluded that a promise has been made. Her romantic delicacy will not allow her to force a confession. I tell her that you have not confided in me. Tell me now, dear. Are you indeed engaged to be married?'

'We have made a promise to write, and he has arranged to follow us to Bath when he has ended Mr. Blake's trial. Perhaps I may thus be reconciled to that dirty, ill-paved city.'

'Jane, you are so provoking,' said Cassie. 'Has Mr. Rose made his intentions clear? Am I to lose you? Believe me when I tell you that there is no gentleman I consider more worthy.'

Jane took her sister's hand. The moon illuminated her sister's face to a waxy paleness.

'My dearest sister. What happiness is mine all around me – slippery, dangerous, blinding happiness! I do believe that he is the only man I could ever love. More I cannot, will not, say. He did not at all urge or press me for an answer and only asked leave to see me often. He has asked to speak to Papa when we meet in Bath. I am perfectly content.'

Cassie was unused to the grave tone in which her sister spoke. She squeezed her hand and then took it to her lips. 'Then I, my dear, am content, too. Every happiness will be yours.'

Tell me you love me, on that my existence depends,
and I never can grow tired of hearing it. I believe I
may say with the most perfect assurance of not
being deceived, that the most amiable and feeling
heart in the world is entirely mine. You may
suppose me agitated; but indeed I am, much more
so than is rational. However, I cannot help it,
Sorrow is more easily to be borne with fortitude
than joy beyond all the hopes I had ever formed.

I without hesitation commit to paper my
sentiments and glory in them. I am under a full and
perfect conviction that time will only add strength
and fervency to them. That every Christmas Day I
may live to see, will find me equally devoted to the
only Being I ever have or ever shall adore.

A tiredness washed over him and he set his pen aside. He
would finish the letter in the morning. The chamber felt
close and sultry. He took his muffler, wrapped it around
his throat and walked out of the stone cottage to the
water's edge. A disabled boat was lying keel upward,
big-bellied. The waves crashed and hissed against the
rocks and then fell silent. A bell clanged noisily in the
distance.

It was the stillest hour of the night, the hour before dawn, when the world seemed to hold its breath, suspended. Salty droplets covered his face. He took out her cambric handkerchief, freshly laundered. The stain had almost disappeared.

The gold watch was ticking, solid and heavy in his hand. His thoughts turned to Blake:

To see a World in a Grain of Sand
And a Heaven in a Wild Flower
Hold Infinity in the palm of your hand
And Eternity in an hour

Safely returned from Colyton and ensconced in Sydney Place, the Austens were awaiting the appointed day for Mr. Rose to make his appearance and be reunited with the family. An exchange of letters had passed between the two, with news of Mr. Blake's impending trial and Rose's eager anticipation of his leave-taking of Sussex. When the conclusion of the session finally arrived, his barouche would be waiting to transport him to Bath.

The house, situated at the western end of Sydney Gardens, possessed a quiet grace that bespoke its unassuming refinement. It was neither striking nor excessively plain. The rooms within were comfortable without being ostentatious, the ceilings adorned with delicate cornices and the walls painted in soft hues. The furniture was well chosen and genteel, including chairs and sofas upholstered in figured damask. A drawing room of good dimensions offered a limited view of the city yet pleased the eye with the orderly charm of nature subdued to the hand of art, enlivened by the comings and goings of those who strolled through the gardens.

September had been ushered in with heavy rainfall and stormy clouds. The chambermaid had lit a fire and the group gathered together in the drawing room. Mrs. Austen had suggested an evening's entertainment of making doggerel verses. They should rhyme with 'Rose', she announced. She volunteered to go first:

This morning I 'woke from a quiet repose,
I first rubbed my eyes and I next blew my nose.
With my Stockings and Shoes I then covered my
toes
And proceeded to put on the rest of my Cloathes.
My flesh is much warmer, my blood freer flows
When I work in the garden with rakes and with
hoes.
And now I believe I must come to a close,
For I find I grow stupid e'en while I compose;
If I write any longer my verse will be prose.

She was greeted with much applause and congratulations. Cassie shyly read aloud her own ditty:

Love, they say is like a Rose;
I'm sure tis like the wind that blows,
For not a human creature knows
How it comes or where it goes.
It is the cause of many woes,
It swells the eyes and reds the nose,
And very often changes those
Who once were friends to bitter foes.
But when the heart has full repose,
'Tis Mutual Love the gift bestows.

'Hurrah,' said Jane to her sister with a mock bow. She trusted that Samuel would admire the verse, which had been composed in his honour. How he would laugh – his voice a throaty baritone. She imagined his delivery in the courtroom for the case for the defence. Such were his powers that the trial would surely go in Mr. Blake's favour.

The only blight on her happiness was a delay in his correspondence due, no doubt, to his engagement with the Assizes.

Later in the evening, Jane began a letter to her brother.

My dearest Frank,

I have much to say, as people usually have when
they begin to talk of themselves. How quick come
the reasons for approving what we like! As to
describing the extreme wish I have for you to learn
to love him – it is in vain to attempt it. I shall not
attempt either to give you any idea of his character;
it is such to ensure my happiness. You must excise
my incoherent and uncomfortable style, dearest, I
am sure you will! You cannot imagine the state of
mind into which the certainty of being preferred
by the person whom reason and inclination greatly
approves, and the prospect of so awful a change of
life and accession of duties, throws me.

Our six weeks by the sea will never be forgotten.
What happiness is mine – all around me. For the
clock is fast wearing away at the minutes to the
happy hour of twelve, when a well-known step
will sound along the passages and a well-known
voice will be heard at my door.

Nothing, my dear Frank, is more unlike a novel
than real life. And perfect happiness, even in memory,
is not common. Happiness is not something that
happens to us, it is something we chose.

Yours affectionately, J A.

Postscript. Miss Lloyd joins us tomorrow for an
extended stay.

It was another Indian summer morning. Jane and Martha rose early, put on their bonnets and stole quietly out of the house. They crossed the road and took a turn round Sydney Gardens, before walking through the city.

Bath was awaking to a cacophony of sounds.

As they strolled along Great Pulteney Street, a sooty chimney boy, with dingy face and tattered clothes, was shouting loudly to advertise his trade, waking up the sleepy housemaids. On Laura Place, a milkman rattled his pail and the dustman's bell clanged. As they crossed the bridge over the river, the air filled with the din of hackney coaches, wagons, carts and tradesmen making their way to work. Along Milsom Street freshly sprinkled water cooled the feet of the early walkers. A ruddy maid twirled her mop, annoying a smartly clad apprentice.

The morning sun shone through shop windows, as canvas awnings were extended to provide shade for the inviting merchandise. Insects buzzed around the tempting pastries and a sticky trap waited to catch them. The lamplighter climbed a tall ladder to extinguish the lamps, while a pot boy yelled discordantly.

Rounding the Circus, they were eyed by an old-clothes man with a bag of half-worn dresses – no doubt pilfered by some dishonest maid – which he was hoping to sell for a fraction of their worth. A porter carried his heavy load along the Royal Crescent.

They walked briskly.

The air was crisp and fresh as Jane and Martha ascended Lansdown Hill, the soft light casting a gentle glow over the city below. Here, they were alone with their thoughts, the world at their feet and the future a murmur just beyond their grasp.

Martha, her bonnet slightly askew, was looking out with a wistful expression.

'Martha,' Jane began, her voice steady but laced with concern, 'you have not said a word since we left the house. I would not intrude upon your thoughts, but I cannot bear to see you in such distress.'

Martha sighed. 'It is only that I fear, Jane, that we may never see Frank again. The war, the sea, the uncertainty of his life.'

Jane reached out, gently taking her hand. 'You must not think so, dear Martha. His duty to the Navy is indeed a heavy burden, but it is also his pride, his honour. He will return to us all. Of that, I am certain.'

'But when?' Martha's voice was unsteady. 'What if it is years, Jane? What if … what if it is never?'

Jane hesitated, her own heart heavy with the uncertainty that had plagued her since leaving Devonshire. She could not offer false comfort, but neither could she stand to see her friend in such despair. 'If it is years, then years you will wait. If it is never ... then ... then you will still have loved him with a constancy that few can claim. But you must not let such thoughts consume you. He will return. He must.'

Martha's eyes filled with tears. 'You are too kind, Jane. You speak of constancy as if it were a virtue, and perhaps it is, but I cannot help but feel that it is a cruel one. To love someone so deeply and to be left in this endless waiting.'

Jane now understood all too well what it was to wait, to hope, to doubt. She gazed down on the city in silence.

'And what of you, Jane?' Martha asked suddenly, as if reading her thoughts. 'You have spoken of my fears, but what of your own? Do you hear from Mr. Rose? Has he written?'

'He was to return to Bath as soon as his case was concluded, but there has been no word. I do not know what to think.'

'Perhaps he is merely delayed,' Martha suggested, though her tone was halting, as if she were trying to convince herself as much as Jane. 'The law is a demanding profession, is it not? Surely, there are matters that require his attention, matters that may have prevented him from writing.'

'Perhaps.'

'He loves you, of that I am certain. He is a man of honour, of integrity. You wrote of how, once before, he left but returned. He would not abandon you.'

'I have written to him, Martha, but there has been no reply. Not a single word.'

'There must be some explanation, something that has prevented him from writing.'

'And if there is not? I am not one to wait forever, Martha.'

'But, Jane, to give up on love? Is that truly what you desire?'

'It is not what I desire,' she admitted. 'But neither can I endure this uncertainty. If he does not return, if he does not make his intentions clear, then I must assume that his feelings have changed. I shall not repine. My tranquillity and peace stand a better chance.'

They fell silent again, until Jane spoke, her tone lighter.

'Come, Martha, let us not dwell on these uncertainties. The day is too fine to be spent in melancholy. Tomorrow may bring better news. And we have each other. And Cassie. Perhaps no man can be a good judge of the comfort a woman feels in the society of her own sex.'

THE TRIAL

*Chichester, Sussex, England,
September 1801.*

On a fitfully wet autumnal day, the Reverend Dr. Youatt takes his place for the Assizes in the Chichester Guildhall. As court recorder, it is his duty to take a shorthand record of the proceedings. Six magistrates are presided over by the Duke of Richmond, who sits beneath a full-length portrait of King George III. The jurymen are to the side of the room.

Mr. William Blake, miniature painter, resident of nearby Felpham, is in attendance to answer the charge of Sedition against His Majesty, his treasonous acts being assault and battery on the person of Private John Scholfield of the Royal Dragoon Guards. It is alleged that he dragged the private through the village, holding him by the collar and throwing him bodily into his barracks, while vehemently uttering the seditious expressions 'Damn the King', 'You Soldiers are all Slaves' and 'If Bonaparte should come he would be master of Europe in an Hour's Time.' There is one witness for the prosecution, Private John Cock, also of the Dragoons. Several witnesses are to be called by counsel for the defence, Mr. Samuel Rose.

In the light of a local rumour that Bonaparte has assembled fleets of flatboats in every creek and harbour on the French side of the Channel, there will be terrible consequences – transportation or worse – in the event of a guilty verdict in a crime against the person of a Dragoon stationed by the coast for the express purpose of defending the nation from this direst of threats.

After the prosecution has presented its case, entirely reliant upon the testimony of Scholfield and Cock, Mr. Samuel Rose rises to put the case for the defence. The Reverend Dr. Youatt sharpens his pen and transcribes. The eloquence of the speech tests his art of shorthand to the full.

'Gentlemen of the Jury,' Rose begins, in a quiet, measured and authoritative voice.

'I perfectly agree with my learned friend for the prosecution, with regard to the atrocity and malignity of the charge of high treason now laid before you. My task is to show that my client is not guilty of the words imputed to him. It is not to show that they are capable of any mitigated sense. We stand here not merely in form, but in sincerity and truth, to declare that we are *not guilty.*'

One of the jurymen nudges his drowsing neighbour. These were words worth listening to.

'Mr. Blake is as loyal a subject as any man in this court: as you have heard, he feels as much indignation at the idea of exposing to contempt or injury the sacred person of his sovereign as any man. Gentlemen, this is a very uncommon accusation. It is foreign to our natures and opposite to our habits. Do you not hear every day from the mouths of thousands in the streets the exclamation of God Save the King? That is the language on every Englishman's lip, the effusion of every Englishman's heart. Gentlemen, the greater the offence charged, the greater the improbability of its being true. I will state to you the situation of Mr. Blake and it will be for you to judge whether it is probable he should be guilty of the crime alleged.'

By now the room is hushed.

'He is an artist, who, though not a native here, has lived in your part of the country for some time. He was brought into this country by Mr. Hayley, a gentleman well known to you, and whose patriotism and loyalty have never been impeached. Blake was previously known to Mr. Hayley. I think I need not state that Mr. Hayley would never have brought Mr. Blake into this part of the country, and given him encouragement, if he conceived it possible that he could have uttered these sentiments. Mr. Hayley from his previous knowledge of him was certain that he was not the seditious character here represented.'

There are murmurs of approval from the public gallery. Eyes turn towards Mr. Hayley, nodding with pleasure in the front row, a most respected member of the community.

'Gentlemen, the story is very improbable, if we further consider Mr. Blake's situation. Mr. Blake is engaged as an engraver. He has a wife to support: that wife and himself he has supported by his art – an art which has a tendency, like all the other fine arts, to soften every asperity of feeling and of character, and to secure the bosom from the influence of those tumultuous and discordant passions which destroy the happiness of mankind. If any men are likely to be exempt from angry passions it is such a one as Mr. Blake.'

One of the jurors, who considers himself an artist, places his hand on his heart.

'The witness Scholfield is in a different situation from what he has been. This man was once a serjeant – he is now a private. He says he was degraded on account of drunkenness. He is degraded, be it from what cause it may – he certainly does not stand before you under the most favourable circumstances, nor is he entitled to that credit which you would have given him, if by his good conduct he had continued in his former situation, or raised himself to a higher.'

Samuel Rose is in full stride, but he feels a weakness in his knees.

'He tells you a story, which to be sure requires a great deal of faith in order to believe it – because it is an unaccountable story. He was in Blake's garden talking to the ostler, that he had but few words to say, and no time to spare, yet we find him lounging about leaning against the garden wall. That Mr. Blake came out, and without any provocation, without one word being spoken on either side, began to utter the words in the indictment. The witness at one time asserted that these words were spoken to him, then he was doubting whether they were addressed to Mrs. Blake – but now he asserts again that they were spoken to him.'

From the corner of his eye, the Reverend Dr. Youatt observes the full rank of jurymen nodding. He has little doubt that the supreme eloquence, patriotism, principle and humanity of Mr. Samuel Rose is winning them over.

'Gentlemen, you will take notice that the ostler was all this time working in the garden – this garden I shall be able to prove to you did not contain above ten yards square – no words consequently could have been uttered without every person in the garden hearing them, especially when Scholfield acknowledged that they were talking rather high. The ostler is allowed to have been in the garden, he was in a situation to hear all that passed, and he will prove to you by and by that he heard no such expressions uttered by Mr. Blake.'

Beads of perspiration are breaking out on Samuel Rose's forehead. I can't go on, I must go on, I shall go on, he says to himself.

A juryman is heard muttering to his neighbour that this Scholfield is manifestly a rogue, whose word cannot be trusted. The Duke of Richmond reprimands him and calls for silence in court. Unflustered without but dizzy within, Rose continues:

'The second witness, Private Cock, states that he saw Mr. Blake and Scholfield in the act of collaring each other. He states that without any further provocation or hearing any words from Scholfield or Blake, Blake uttered these words, damn the King, damn the country, you soldiers are all slaves. I shall call a further witness who will state that she was as near Mr. Blake as Cock was, and *heard no such words*. You shall hear her account – you will then agree with me that it totally overthrows the testimony of these soldiers.'

The Reverend Dr. Youatt senses that there is not a man in the courtroom who could fail to be impressed by Mr. Samuel Rose's forensic evisceration of the case for the prosecution.

But at this moment there is a commotion.

Seemingly overcome by a sudden illness, Rose falls to the floor in a faint.

Fading away.

The proceedings are halted while he is revived with smelling salts and removed to the fresh air of the street.

The Duke of Richmond spends several minutes in conclave with the six magistrates. What is to be done? In the absence of counsel, the witnesses for the defence cannot be called. But such has been the strength of the case presented by Rose that to rule for adjournment and a retrial will be a waste of time during the busy Assize season. The jury is accordingly instructed to retire and consider their verdict on the basis of all that they have heard.

They do not deliberate for long.

The Dragoons are not popular. The public gallery erupts in cheers of approval upon the delivery of a unanimous verdict. Not guilty.

Hayley, meanwhile, has rushed from the Guildhall and engaged a private carriage to return Samuel Rose to London for an immediate consultation with his doctor.

As he helps him into the post chaise, which is to be pulled by a pair of sturdy black Percherons, he is able to say, 'My dear, dear friend, such was the power of your words that we have gained our cause. Blake is acquitted. Posterity will remember you for this.'

THE SECOND SHOCK

4 Sydney Place, Bath, England,
1 October 1801.

Autumn had arrived, and there was still no word from Mr. Rose. Nor had he visited at his appointed date. Her letters had gone unanswered. Nor had she heard a word about the outcome of the trial. All was silent. She missed the companionship of Martha, who had returned to Hampshire.

One chilly morning, a parcel arrived. Jane tore it open and saw a letter written in a stranger's hand. She read the opening line:

To Miss Jane Austen,
I write with the most melancholy of news …

She could read no more without Cassie by her side. She called out for her and thrust the package into her sister's hands.

'Pray, my dear, read it to me. I am composed.'

Cassie was all astonishment and scoured the letter for the writer's name.

'It is Mr. Hayley, Jane. Are you acquainted with the gentleman?'

'No, not at all – though, as you know, I admire his works.'

As Cassie read on, Jane was only half-conscious of the words spoken.

Prospects of a brilliant future were only dashed
by wavering health. On that sunken rock, how
many struggling in the same arduous career –
often those of brightest promise, of finest nature
– have been wrecked, almost at the outset; not
great and famous, but nameless and
unremembered.

'Sit down, my dear. I shall fetch my mother and father.'
'Read on.'

As you know only too well, madam, in the course
of the summer he tried the air of the Devonshire
coast, where he was so invigorated by both the
benefits of sea bathing and the elegant, conducive
society of other sojourners that he appeared to
recover his health entirely. It is, alas, the nature of
the subtle disease with which he was afflicted, to
elude the observation of its victim in a very

marvellous manner, and Rose is a remarkable example of this consolatory truth.

Jane held her breath.

When he visited us at Felpham to meet Mr. Blake and prepare his brief, I was so shocked by his emaciated appearance that I earnestly entreated him to suspend his hazardous intention of continuing to take every worthy case that was offered him; but impaired as he was in bodily strength, his mind retained all its energy without a particle of apprehension. He had established it as a law, never to shrink from any professional duty, and he fell an early victim to that magnanimous resolution. Even as his disorder assumed new shapes and gradually occasioned a great variety of sufferings, he had no perception of his own danger.

Jane's eyes were filling with tears, but she held them back, forcing herself to think only of his fortitude.

Indeed, he confided in me that he was forming very cheerful plans of future occupation and, he intimated, even of matrimonial prospects. In despite of his failing health, he exercised his faculties to the full in the dispatch of the business of defending Mr. Blake against that malicious and unfounded charge of Sedition. His opening speech was a masterpiece of advocacy, though in a moment of high drama, causing much consternation in the courtroom, he collapsed with exhaustion before its conclusion.

'Is he dead?' said Jane. 'Of what cause?'
Cassie continued to read.

As a result of this great increase of debility, through my offices he was instantly returned to London, where he drew from his physician, Dr. Farr, a perfect avowal of his imminent danger. He heard it with surprise, but without any emotions of terror or dismay. His decline, we fear, was so rapid that he was not able even to inform his nearest and dearest of his imminent demise. Aware that he must now, in all probability, have very few days to live, with serene magnanimity he exclusively deployed them in the most earnest yet tranquil attention to all the duties of a departing Christian. The death of Addison himself, so distinguished by Christian serenity, and so feelingly recorded by the poet Young, affords not a scene of more instruction than the departure of Rose; of whom, though his life had the grace of the most becoming benevolence, it may be truly said, in the words of Shakespeare,

Nothing in his life
Became him like the leaving it: he died
As one, that had been studied in his death.
I write this with the greatest regret, but I remain, madam,

Your most obedient servant
William Hayley

'Consumption,' said Jane. 'That is why he was at Sidmouth. And he never spoke a word of it to me.'

'There are further enclosures,' said Cassie, handing her sister an unfinished letter, a blood-stained handkerchief and a heavy velvet case containing a gold watch, still ticking like the beat of a heart.

Jane, with composure, placed the parcel on the side table. She sank slowly to the floor.

Falling away.

Spinning, whirling, tilting, and yet everything in the room is deathly still.

Falling away.

THE RECOLLECTION

Newton Newbury, Hampshire,
England, 1828.

M r. Henry Edridge of the Engineers was a very pleasant gentleman, unusually gifted with all that was agreeable. Cassandra was quite taken with him. Indeed, she found him consuming her thoughts when she least expected, first thing in the morning and last thing at night. Yes, a most attractive person. It had been a long time since she had seen someone with such a pleasing address, and manners, and so well-bred.

Caroline Austen found her aunt unusually pensive and not at all her cheerful self. Now in her sixth decade, Aunt Cass was a pale, dark-eyed lady with a high arched nose and a kind smile. She was dressed in a long black cloak and a straw bonnet made of black satin. On the index finger of her left hand, she wore a mourning ring set with pearls. She carried a gold watch on a twisted gold chain. She was never seen without them. The morning was drawing to a close and she sat in her chair, twisting her pearl ring, clearly moved by the young man, and troubled.

Caroline sat patiently.

When her aunt finally spoke, the words came flooding out. Mr. Edridge bore an uncommon resemblance to a young man she and her sister had known many years ago. It was in the year 1801, shortly after they had been turned out of their family home and relocated to Bath, which had been such a dreadful shock to her sister.

While their lodgings were being renovated, the family had removed to Devonshire for six weeks by the sea. It was there they had met the young gentleman. He seemed greatly attracted to Aunt Jane. It had been an intercourse of some weeks, but they had to part. He was urgent to know if he could visit her in Bath when his business permitted, and they had begun a correspondence.

Aunt Cass said that he had fallen in love with Jane and was quite in earnest.

'His charm of person, mind and manners made him worthy to possess my sister's love. His suit would have been successful, but then came a letter with news of his sudden demise.'

Through all of the long, lonely years without her sister she had buried the memory of the young man and, with her memory failing, she had forgotten his name. But now, meeting Mr. Henry Edridge, it was as though he were before her. As though she were seeing him for the first time, making his bow and requesting her sister's hand for the dance. And, so too, she remembered that summer in Devonshire, so long ago, when the breeze was soft and warm, and the voice of the sea seductive and inviting and her sister was truly in love, for the only time in her short life.

'So Aunt Jane did not get her own happy ending?'

'Yes, I do believe she did. But not in the common manner. I recall a conversation, a few months after the gentleman's death. It went a little like this.'

'There are no happy endings,' I said to Jane, 'just look around you.'

'There are in novels.'

'Only in novels.'

'Then all of my novels will have happy endings.'

AUTHOR'S AFTERWORD

One of the questions I am most frequently asked about Jane Austen is 'Did she ever fall in love?' Surely, people say, the world's most famous and beloved author of romantic novels – the creator of Elizabeth Bennet and Mr. Darcy, Anne Elliot and Captain Wentworth – *must* once have been in love herself?

This is the starting point of *Six Weeks by the Sea*, a fiction underpinned by many historical and biographical facts. Jane Austen had several potential love interests during her lifetime but chose to remain single. She accepted one marriage proposal from a family friend, only to reject the offer the following morning.

Many believe that Jane Austen's only love was Tom Lefroy, the charming Irish barrister with whom she began a flirtation when she was nineteen. It would, however, seem that, though they were attracted to one another, it was a first crush rather than a lasting love.

After he returned to Ireland, she wrote about him in a light-hearted, not a heartbroken, manner.

The more interesting candidate for winning Jane Austen's heart was an unknown man whom she met at the Devonshire seaside resort of Sidmouth in the summer of 1801, when she was twenty-five.

Many years after her sister's death, Cassandra Austen met a young man who was a friend of her nephew, Edward Austen-Leigh. His name was Henry Edridge, an officer in the Corps of Royal Engineers. Cassandra was greatly taken with the handsome young man and was saddened to hear the news of his sudden death a short time after their first meeting. The incident reminded her of another handsome young man whom she had met at Sidmouth years before in the company of her sister, Jane.

Cassandra explained to her niece Caroline that this young man was deeply attracted to Jane, and she to him. That a seaside romance was formed, and that the young man asked to meet up with the family later in the summer. According to Caroline Austen's account of this conversation, he had fallen in love with Jane and was quite in earnest: 'I never heard Aunt Cass. speak of anyone else with such admiration – she had no doubt that a mutual attachment was in progress between him and her sister. They parted – but he made it clear that he would seek them out again – and shortly afterwards he died.' Another family version of the story adds that instead of his expected arrival, a letter came announcing his death.

Cassandra would have been particularly affected by this, because her own sole love, Tom Fowle, a former pupil of her father's to whom she was engaged, died of yellow fever when accompanying his patron to the West Indies.

Over the years, some of the Austen family members confused the unnamed seaside admirer with another would-be suitor, a clergyman and Cambridge don called the Reverend Dr. Samuel Blackall. Jane Austen's friend Anne Lefroy (who was also involved in the Tom Lefroy debacle) was keen to promote a match between Jane and Blackall. After he had met Jane in 1798, Blackall told Anne that he would have to wait some years before becoming financially secure. Jane wrote to Cassandra about the abortive affair: 'I am very well satisfied it will all go on exceedingly well, and decline away in a very reasonable manner ... our indifference will soon be mutual, unless his regard, which appeared to spring from knowing nothing of me at first, is best supported by never seeing me.' Hardly a ringing endorsement.

Nevertheless, Jane kept up an interest in Blackall, and when he finally married in 1813 she noted the fact to her brother Frank, who was clearly well aware of the situation: 'I wonder whether you happened to see Mr. Blackall's marriage in the papers last January? We did.' She went on to describe him with her characteristic irony as a 'piece of Perfection, noisy Perfection'. She also expressed a desire to know more about his bride, Miss

Lewis, hoping that she would be 'fond of cold veal pies, green tea in the afternoon, and a green window blind at night'. The Reverend Dr. Blackall, who lived a long if dull life, was clearly *not* the mystery man whom Jane Austen met at the seaside and whose court-ship was so tragically cut short by his sudden, premature death.

Jane Austen's other great love was the sea.

When her parents announced in December 1800 that they were leaving the family home of Steventon and retiring to Bath, Jane was so shocked that she fainted. As she explained in a letter to Cassandra, she reconciled herself to the move only when the family promised to take a holiday by the seaside every summer:

I get more and more reconciled to the idea of our removal. We have lived long enough in this neighborhood: the Basingstoke balls are certainly on the decline, there is something interesting in the bustle of going away, and the prospect of spending future summers by the sea is very delightful. For a time we shall now possess many of the advantages which I have often thought of with envy in the wives of sailors or soldiers.

So it was that in 1801 and 1802 they went to Sidmouth and Teignmouth in Devonshire. In 1803 and 1804 it was the turn of Lyme Regis, which, years later, would be the setting of her final and most wistful completed novel, *Persuasion*.

Sidmouth, a lovely, unspoilt seaside town, nestles beneath majestic red cliffs and the green hills of the glorious Sid Valley. Austen, always a keen walker, could climb up the Peak Hill and see the panoramic views of its long, golden beaches. The sea at Sidmouth is a shimmering blue and pink, a peculiar effect of the reflection from the cliffs and sand. In my imagination, the blood-red sea became a metaphor for the consumption that is slowly killing Samuel Rose.

The inns and lodging houses were set on the wide sweeping esplanade, known as the Mall, to command the finest sea views. The soft, clear air and its temperate climate added to its attractions and led to the reputation of this part of the coast as the English Riviera. The long war with France meant that visitors flocked to the English seaside where they could enjoy the 'fashionable rage for sea bathing'. Jane Austen greatly enjoyed being dipped in the sea and it was pleasing to imagine her splashing about in the waves.

The Austens were invited to east Devon at the request of Richard Buller, one of George Austen's Steventon pupils, who was newly wed and settled in the village of Colyton, where he was vicar. Colyton, with its magnificent rural views, nestles between Sidmouth in Devonshire and Lyme Regis and Charmouth in Dorsetshire, making it an ideal location from which to make a tour of the seaside.

In order to recreate some of the local detail and colour of the Devonshire seaside, I was fortunate to find an edition in four volumes of John Swete's marvellous illustrated journals, *Travels in Georgian Devon: 1789–1800*. The reverend's eccentric character – he was a watercolourist who travelled around Devonshire on his donkey (reminiscent of cartoonist Thomas Rowlandson's famous character Dr. Syntax!) – became an inspiration for a key player in my novel. He suddenly sprang to life one day, and the journals provided me with a fund of irresistible catchphrases and pomposities worthy of one of Jane Austen's own characters. The Reverend Swete's palatial home, Oxton House in Devonshire, thus became the setting of an important scene, and the details of the house and its lush gardens, newly landscaped by 'Capability' Brown, were sourced from his journals.

One of the most important characters for this novel was Jane's naval brother Francis William Austen, who was the model for midshipman William Price in *Mansfield Park* and Captain Harville in *Persuasion*. He was only a year older than Jane: brother and sister were extremely close. A gifted craftsman, he made Jane a beautiful, carved wooden letter case. Over his long career aboard ship, and through his many adventures and dangers at sea, Frank saved and cherished every single letter sent by his sister, though after his death the majority of them were destroyed by his youngest daughter, Fanny Sophia.

Frank was an avid correspondent. Like William Price, who was away at sea for a period of five years, letters from home were a lifeline for a sailor. It seems clear that Frank spoke openly about his experiences on board ship, including references to sailors who were flogged for homosexuality. Jane Austen's sexually risqué joke in *Mansfield Park*, with its reference to *Rears* and *Vices* (her italics), makes her understanding of sodomy in the Navy evident.

The character of Captain Peter Parker was loosely based on a real naval figure, who was not, however, homosexual in real life. In my novel his sexual orientation, in those days illegal and punishable by death, became a conduit by which to explore the dangers and difficulties of living a closeted life. The two Hampshire sailors hanged for sodomy in 1801 was a true story taken from a newspaper of the time.

Martha Lloyd, Jane Austen's closest friend, was in love with Frank Austen, and Jane's wish was for them to unite in marriage. Frank eventually married, but, many years after Jane's death, and the death of his first wife, he did indeed marry Martha. She became Lady Austen and they lived together in his mansion in Portsmouth overlooking the sea. I used the details of Martha Lloyd's household book to add colour to her character, such as her recipe for Indian curry, beloved by Frank.

The character of Leah, the biracial granddaughter of Reverend Swete is entirely imaginary. However, Lady

Sarah Brocas of Wokefield Park is based on a real person, the biracial daughter of an Antiguan planter and an enslaved woman. Named Sarah Redhead, she married Bernard Brocas, who was the heir to two stately homes, Wokefield Park in Berkshire and Beaurepaire in Hampshire, a mansion close to the Austen family home. The Brocas family was well known to the Austen family, not least because another of Jane's brothers was vicar of their parish. The fabulous wrought-iron gates, designed by Sir John Soane, did indeed bear the insignia of two African men wearing coronets. They were eventually transferred from Wokefield Park to Beaurepaire.

A biracial woman marrying into an aristocratic family in Georgian England was by no means as unusual as is often assumed. Miss Georgiana Lambe, Austen's own biracial character in *Sanditon*, the novel on which she was working when she died, is also wealthy and sought after as an eligible bride. The seaside holidays were, of course, a major inspiration for both *Persuasion* and *Sanditon*.

Jane Austen's support for the abolitionist movement is clear from her admiration for the leading campaigner Thomas Clarkson and from references in *Mansfield Park* and *Emma*. In my novel, one of the reasons she is drawn to the mysterious stranger is his support for the abolition of the slave trade. My interest in this theme arose from the commission to write the tie-in book to *Belle*, the award-winning 2013 movie about Dido Belle, the biracial girl, daughter of an enslaved woman, who was taken in and raised at Kenwood House by Lord Chief Justice Mansfield, whose rulings in the epoch-making Somerset v. Stewart and *Zong* slave ship cases spurred the abolition. In that book, I demonstrated that, through a Kentish family connection, Jane would have known the extraordinary story of Dido's upbringing.

My depiction of the elusive Jane Austen has been influenced by years of writing and thinking about her life and works. Her letters provided some of the inspiration for her characteristic wit and playfulness, alongside the lively ladies of the stage and page in whose tradition she stands: Lady G. of Samuel Richardson's *Sir Charles Grandison*, Lady Delacour of Maria Edgeworth's *Belinda* and Mrs. Candour of Richard Brinsley Sheridan's *The School for Scandal* (a character whom Jane once represented in family theatricals), not to mention her witty and brilliant cousin, Eliza.

Edgeworth's fine novel *Belinda* was indeed published in the summer of 1801, licensing my scene in which Jane and her suitor bond over their admiration for it. *Belinda* was controversial for its depiction of a marriage between a white woman and a man of colour; I was also inspired by an excellent but little-known novel of 1808 called *The Woman of Colour*.

Finally, the hero of my story was based upon a real individual, a gentleman by the name of Samuel Rose. He was a brilliant and charismatic lawyer, who was also deeply interested in literature. He edited the *Miscellaneous Works* of Oliver Goldsmith. He was the dear friend of both William Cowper, Jane Austen's best-loved poet, and another of her favourite authors, William Hayley. Thanks to Hayley's good offices, Rose became the friend and advocate of the poet and artist William Blake. I made his defence of Blake in the latter's trial for sedition a key element of my plot. The trial in fact took place in 1804 – I have used artistic licence to transpose it to 1801.

At the time of the Chichester trial, Samuel Rose was dying from tuberculosis. He had recently been recuperating from an illness at the seaside, bathing in the ocean and taking the waters (in real life, at a different resort – Margate on the Kentish coast, where that other tuberculosis victim John Keats would also take refuge). Coughing up blood, paleness of complexion and glittering (feverish) eyes are some of the symptoms of consumption that I explore in the novel. During the Blake trial, Mr. Rose collapsed. Within the year, he was dead. Details of the trial and Rose's final hours were adapted from the court reporter's transcript and an account of his death in the monthly literary periodical *European Magazine and London Review*.

Though the real-life Samuel Rose was not the Sidmouth stranger, he was the inspiration for my hero. With his eloquence, his love of literature and his steadfast Christian faith, he seemed to me the type of gentleman who could indeed capture the affection, respect and love of a woman such as Jane Austen. It seems probable that her mystery man died of a similar disease to consumption, perhaps one of the reasons he was seeking the sea-bathing cure at Sidmouth!

Had it not been for the death of Henry Edridge, the story of Jane Austen's true romance would have been lost to posterity, like a footprint in the sand washed away by the waves.